DECEPTION

Playboy Danton Rhodes preys on rich women, squandering their fortunes before the inevitable divorce. He never expected to fall in love with Lois Carter, a married woman with a watertight prenuptial agreement; but when he learns that Lois's stepdaughter Dee needs to marry before her next birthday in order to receive her inheritance, Danton smells an opportunity. As Dee's cousin Helen arrives at the family home, she finds chaos — Lois has been violently attacked, and the suspect is none other than the familiar face she picked up along the way . . .

V. J. BANIS

DECEPTION

Complete and Unabridged

LINFORD
Leicester

First published in Great Britain

First Linford Edition
published 2020

A catalogue record for this book is available
from the British Library.

ISBN 978–1–4448–4373–6

Published by
F. A. Thorpe (Publishing)
Anstey, Leicestershire

Set by Words & Graphics Ltd.
Anstey, Leicestershire
Printed and bound in Great Britain by
T. J. International Ltd., Padstow, Cornwall

This book is printed on acid-free paper

1

Danton Rhodes was well known as a playboy. And a womanizer. The latter had started when he had been a lad, and had involved of necessity, older women, which is to say, women who were more likely to be amenable to sexual advances from a young man than were the young ladies of his own age.

He had over the years become quite adept at what he thought of (although he had more sense than to say this aloud) as 'managing' women. After all, as he had laughingly said often, if only to himself, you learned more about women from women than you can learn from girls.

At the age of eighteen he had inherited a sizable amount of money from a trust fund established by his grandparents. That money had soon vanished, most of it spent on the proverbial wine, women and song, the emphasis on the middle component. He was fond of saying he was not much of a wine drinker, his preference being for scotch, and he had rarely been known to break into song (and on those few occasions when he had done so most listeners declared themselves grateful for the rarity) but women . . . ah, women were the principle joy of his life.

At the still tender age of twenty-two, he had found himself once again strapped for money. Undaunted, he had solved that problem by marrying the first of his several wives, a woman of thirty odd years (she was vague about saying exactly how many) and a couple of million dollars.

By the time he was thirty, that wife had divorced him. The divorce, alas, came too late to prevent his wasting her fortune in much the same way as his own. Being married did not in any way interfere with his interest in women — many women.

The same pattern with very little variation had prevailed with wives two, three and four. These interludes saw him to his mid-forties, though still handsome and youthful looking; and found him once again close to, if not exactly, penniless.

It was at this juncture in his life when something happened he had never experienced before: he fell in love — or, at least, as much in love as he was capable of falling, with anyone other than himself.

Even stranger, considering his record, was that the woman for whom he had developed this grand and heretofore never known emotion was neither a wealthy woman nor a prospective bride, because she was already married when he met her and began what turned out to be a seriously ardent relationship.

It was true, Lois Carter's husband was a man of some means, but it seemed highly unlikely that Danton might by his usual methods get his hands on Douglas Carter's fortune. Even if the couple were to divorce, they had signed before their wedding prenuptial agreements stating that if the marriage came to an end, she would subsequently get enough to live on, but no more than that, and only until such a time as she might remarry, at which point the money ended.

All was not, however, entirely hopeless. It took Mr. Rhodes hardly any time at all before he had become acquainted with the fact that Douglas Carter had a daughter from his late first wife, and that this particular daughter, who was her father's favorite and whose name was Dee, stood to inherit a sizable amount of money from her late mother, but with one stipulation: she must be married on her fast-approaching twenty-first birthday.

Danton was well versed in the art of marrying; moreover, once he had taken these women to their marital beds, it had never proven any kind of difficulty for him to gain control as well of whatever fortunes they possessed. Had he not squandered several by this juncture in his life? He assumed that the same general circumstances would prevail with the prospective heiress. Who was, after all, little more than a girl, a mere child.

It never crossed his mind that his mistress Lois's stepdaughter, might be any more impervious to his blandishments than the older women of the world to whom he had been previously married.

So, then the answer was a simple one: marry the girl and use her money to finance his ongoing romance with her stepmother.

That this idea might be objectionable to either of the two females involved had never crossed his mind. Both of them, as he saw it, were getting the object of their desires. And if he had even contemplated the matter he would have concluded that there was easily enough 'object' to go around.

It remained, then, only for him to marry the one, and convince the other of the wisdom of his schemes. After all, he was prepared to argue, his marriage to the stepdaughter meant that he and the stepmother could soon afford the relative luxury of motel rooms, instead of waiting for the off chance that the husband would be away from home for an hour or two of an afternoon. Motel rooms cost money, of which he had only a limited supply at the moment.

With this in mind, he had paid a visit to the Carter home in Burbank, not so far away from his modest apartment in the Wilshire district of Los Angeles. He was relieved to see that Douglas Carter's car was not parked in front, where he usually left it when he came home from work. The chances were good that 'the coast was clear.'

★ ★ ★

A day earlier:

'But why do you have to go?' Gemma asked.

'I just do,' the young man said.

'You still have not told me where you are going,' she pointed out.

He gave her a long, measuring look. 'That's right,' he said. 'I haven't.'

'Is it a secret?'

'Gemma, I think we have rather gotten past the stage of keeping secrets from one another. Wouldn't you say?'

'I thought we had,' she said.

'I'm going out,' he said. 'That's all there is to it. I am going out. I'll be back in a day or two. I don't know why you're making such a big thing out of this.' He was seized by a sudden coughing spell, so violent that he looked for a few seconds as if he might pass out. He took hold of the back of a chair, to steady himself. After a moment or two, the coughing fit passed. He held on to the chair and took several deep breaths.

'Because of that, maybe,' she said.

He smiled ruefully at her. 'It won't be any better if I stay here,' he said. 'Some things don't change. This is one of them.'

'It *will* be better if you're here,' she said vehemently. 'I can look after you. If you're somewhere else how can I do anything? Especially if I don't even know where you are?'

'You know I don't want looking after,' he said.

'I know you are as stubborn as a mule,' she said.

He grinned at that. 'You're right. I am. I always have been.'

He had been shoving things into a duffel bag while they talked. Now he zipped it up. 'Well,' he said, and looked hesitantly in her direction. 'Goodbye then.' He was weighing whether he should kiss her or not.

'That sounds so final,' she said.

'It's not. Not yet, anyway. In time, of

course . . . ' he let that remark dangle. They both knew where it was leading. He decided against kissing her. It would not do to invest the moment with any more importance than it already had.

He settled for nodding his head in her direction. He lifted the duffel bag from the surface of the bed and went out the front door, feeling her eyes on his back as he went.

The air outside smelled good and the day promised to be a fine one. There was a bit of a breeze and a tall palm tree by the street stirred in sympathy with the breeze. He walked as far as the bus stop on the corner and stepped to the curb to look up and down the street, just in case.

He had actually never seen a bus at this stop. Maybe it was a ruse, intended to lure foolish travelers into waiting for a bus that would never come. This was Los Angeles, after all, or a part of it. Everyone had cars. You saw them by the hundreds, every day on the freeway.

He was surely the only one in this vast city who did not have a car. Even Gemma had a battered old Chevy which she drove to the supermarket. If he had asked, she would almost have certainly agreed to drive him; but then she would have known where he was going. And that was not likely to please her. He thought it wiser to make his own way, even if he had to walk. He thought about walking. How much time would it take?

Time had changed for him, in ways both big and small. It used to be he would awaken with the first light of dawn, and lie abed for a few minutes, savoring the warmth, the comfort, looking forward hopefully to what a new day would bring. Then, it was up and to the bathroom, brushing one's teeth, getting ready for the day's new adventures.

Now, he was more likely to awaken in the middle of the night, if he slept at all. And when he looked forward to the coming day, there was no hope in it. Nor prospect of adventures.

He wondered about walking once again.

★   ★   ★

In Burbank, Mrs. Ricketts, the house-keeper, was in the kitchen when the front doorbell sounded, busily stirring some-thing in a pot on the stove. And in any case, she was reported to be hard of hearing. Which meant, it was supposed by the others that she probably would not even hear the doorbell.

Lois Tyler Carter, the wife of the house, was in the front parlor, stewing over a problem that had recently come to her attention. Lois had hardly even arrived at the house two years earlier as a bride before she had correctly assessed the house-hold situation. Her then new husband, Douglas, though hardly even aware he had an older daughter, Annie, was slav-ishly devoted to his youngest child, Dee.

The housekeeper, Mrs. Ricketts, a for-midable presence to say the least, was also devoted to Dee. The grandmother, Mr. Carter's mother, who might have offered a counter-balancing force, was on her way to senility.

And Annie? Annie seemed to be of hardly any consequence at all, to anybody in the family.

All of this the new bride had ascertained in her first week or so in the house. As a result of this clear-eyed assessment of how things stood, Lois could not exactly have been said to prostrate herself at Dee's feet, nor at those of the housekeeper, but she was careful all the same to avoid crossing swords with either of them. Which, as she saw it, was just good common sense. She was a woman well aware of where and how her bread was buttered.

Had she suspected even for a moment that Dee, now a young woman, had her eye on the playboy Danton Rhodes, a man twice her age and several times married before, Lois, who by this time had come to realize that her husband was ineffectual in so many ways and certainly in the bedroom, would never have settled on Danton for her own lover.

Douglas Carter had soon been cuckolded: Danton Rhodes and Lois Tyler Carter were lovers. It was unfortunately not until that relationship had already been well established that Lois even came to realize that young Dee, already at age almost-twenty-one having been once married herself, borne a child and divested herself of both, had set her eyes on Danton Rhodes. At least until that inheritance was settled. After that, well . . .

And then that doorbell gave its fateful ring. Being then the closest to the front door, Lois answered the summons.

And whom should she find on the doorstep outside when she flung the door open but the very person about whom she had been fuming angrily if silently for the last half an hour or more: Danton Rhodes.

'Hi, sweetheart,' he greeted her with a smile.

'Sweetheart?' Lois took a step back and raised an angry eyebrow. 'Do you have me confused with Dee, perhaps?'

'What an odd thing to say,' he said. He came inside, closing the door after himself, and looked cautiously in the direction of the stairs going up. 'And unfair, in my opinion.'

'He's not here, if that's who you're looking for,' she said, meaning her husband, Doug. 'He's working late. Again.'

'In that case,' he said, looking relieved, 'I have no idea what you think you know, my darling, but let me put your mind at ease.'

He came to where Lois was standing and took her in his arms. At first she was stiff and resisted his embrace, but when he lowered his mouth to hers, she welcomed it with a sigh of surrender, and her arms came up about his broad shoulders. She told herself she could not resist the man.

'Oh, Danton,' she murmured, and kissed him back with increasing ardor. After a moment, she drew away from him slightly and looked up into his eyes, her expression caustic. 'You do realize, don't you, that she is half your age?'

'Who?' he asked in mock innocence.

'Who? Oh, you . . . ' She gave his broad chest a jab with her fist, and reached up on tiptoe to kiss him again.

He welcomed the kiss until there was an angry squeal from the stairs behind them and he jerked away from the woman in his arms and turned his head to see the girl 'half his age,' the girl he had planned on marrying, standing there, having danced down the stairs and stopped halfway.

She froze where she was, staring down aghast at the two of them, locked as they were in a torrid embrace.

'Danton, you beast,' Dee Carter shrieked at him, her eyes flashing sparks. 'After all those romantic things you said to me. And we are supposed to be getting married in the near future. Have you completely forgotten?'

Lois, who usually was careful to make no waves where her stepdaughter was concerned, was herself sufficiently afire at the moment to be emboldened to utter a harsh cackle of a laugh.

'You silly goose,' she fairly spat. 'He is never going to marry you.'

'Do you think for one moment he would rather have you, you old hag?' Dee demanded angrily. She rushed the rest of the way down the stairs and seizing a pale lavender-colored urn from off the pedestal that stood at the foot of them, she struck her stepmother a violent blow on the head with it.

Both Lois and shards of lavender pottery fell to the carpeted floor

14

2

Dee's mother, Paula, had rather liked the young Marine Dee had married some time back. When she had changed her will to specify that Dee must be married to inherit the money, she had simply supposed that Dee and Gavin would remain married. Paula had come from a Catholic family that did not favor divorce.

Of course, when Dee's husband had attacked her, and ended up in a mental hospital, things were different. No one had voiced any objections then to a divorce.

In the time since, Dee had met Danton Rhodes. And since Dee had to be married to collect all that money, she had decided that Rhodes, an agreeable sort of man with enough good sense to let her have her way in most things, was the perfect partner for her.

He was inclined to agree. The young woman who had set her eyes on him was an attractive one. The money Dee was due to inherit on their marriage only made her doubly attractive in his greedy eyes.

Which left but one impediment to their happy future: the woman who was already his mistress, Lois.

Mrs. Ricketts, the maid, was nowhere near as hard of hearing as she sometimes affected.

So of course she had indeed heard the ring of the doorbell earlier; but since she knew Lois was in the front room and since the ringing of the doorbell was not repeated, she rightly supposed Lois had answered the door herself. Nonetheless, Mrs. Ricketts, never one to leave things to chance, went to the swinging door that connected to the dining room and pressed her ear against the door.

Yes, she heard voices coming from the front of the house. She even heard, in fact, what they were saying. She clicked her tongue and nodded her head, smiling to herself.

And what, she wondered, would Mrs. Carter do to keep her husband from learning about this conversation? Mrs. Ricketts was a woman who liked to have any ammunition she could get to hand to further whatever plans she might make, although just at the moment she hadn't any. Besides which, she did not much like the second wife anyway. Never had, if she were to be honest with herself.

She had not known the first wife. Paula Carter had died before she was hired. The widower seemed to mourn the inconvenience rather more than his loss of a companion and helpmate.

And there was the daughter to be considered. Well, two daughters, actually, but Annie, the younger one, was so retiring, such a quiet little thing, that Mrs. Ricketts often forgot she was even there.

Everyone adored Dee; most especially her father adored her. And Ricketts, always with an eye on the main chance, had realized from the moment she set foot inside the house that the older daughter was really her ticket to ride and had since treated Dee accordingly. They had over time become something far more than family member and servant; they had become intimates, almost friends. Mrs. Ricketts was devoted to Dee.

Satisfied that she had heard enough of the conversation in the front of the house, Ricketts had just turned away from the swinging door, when she heard Dee scream.

The housekeeper froze. She had expected trouble between those two for some time now, stepmother and stepdaughter; and over a man, yet; which in her mind was the silliest thing of all, but women did fight over them. She knew of course about the marriage plans between Dee and Danton Rhodes, and she knew as well about Lois Carter's little romance with the same man. Sooner or later Miss Dee was going to learn the sordid truth.

So fireworks had always been inevitable. To her way of thinking, Danton Rhodes was not worth the bother. No man was, in her opinion.

Always on the lookout for anything that endangered her own security, Ricketts had from the first pegged him as a threat. But one, she felt confident, that she could manage, as need be.

So, she was inclined to let the two women fight it out. It would likely do them both good, and if they rid her of the problem of Mr. Rhodes, so much the better. But she did not have to hear much of the quarrel that ensued to know that things were not working out the way she had hoped they might. Especially when she heard the urn shatter, and something that sounded uncomfortably like a body falling to the floor. She dashed to the rescue.

'Angel, angel, what's wrong, what's happened?' she cried, and pushed her way through the swinging door, to discover that Lois Carter was indeed on the floor and at the moment, Dee was astride the unconscious body, banging her stepmother's bloody head again and again on the square of wooden floor at the foot of the stairs. In the meanwhile, an ineffectual Danton Rhodes stood by looking horror-struck and wringing his manicured hands.

'There, there, lamb,' Ricketts crooned, taking the panting Dee by the shoulders and physically lifting her to her feet.

'That's enough, now. You must stop and catch your breath before you hurt yourself, my darling one.'

'Is she . . . ?' Rhodes asked, staring in horror at the bloodied woman on the floor.

Ricketts knelt by the fallen body to check for a pulse. 'She's alive,' she said. 'But unconscious.' She looked at the blood on her own and Dee's hands, and grimaced. 'Dee, love, you must go up to your room, quickly now,' she ordered. 'And take a shower.'

'It was him,' Dee exclaimed, her eyes flashing maniacally. 'I didn't do it. It was him.'

'But . . . ' Rhodes started to object. 'Him, who? Surely, you don't mean me, I hope.'

'Lamby love,' Ricketts addressed Dee, 'you had a letter just a day or so ago from your first husband, Mr. Gavin, didn't you tell me that? Didn't he say he was coming for a visit. We'll tell everyone he was here, that you saw him running away. They'll believe he did it if we stick to our story.'

'And you,' Ricketts said, fixing Rhodes

with an evil stare, 'you will say nothing. You were not even here, in fact. Do you understand what I am telling you? Otherwise, you are as guilty as anyone. You are a party to the assault on this poor woman. If they arrest us for this, I will see that you share our fate. Do you hear me? Go now, at once, and forget you were ever here.'

Rhodes went, quickly. A minute later, they heard the sound of his car's engine coming to life, and then the squeal of tires as he sped down the driveway.

Which left Dee, still staring in horror from the foot of the stairs, her hands dripping blood.

'Now, lamb,' Ricketts said, having had a moment or two to think things out, 'You do as I told you and go on up to your room and take a shower. Don't worry about any of this. I'll clean stuff up that needs to be cleaned. That vase, for instance, I think we will just get rid of all that, what's left of it. To be honest, I never liked it anyway.'

'Yes, yes,' Dee said breathlessly, still in a daze.

'I'll say I broke the urn while I was dusting. Who's to say I didn't, if I confess.'

'You broke it,' Dee said. 'While you were dusting.'

'I most certainly did. And threw away the pieces. Just you remember what I told you. You were not down here at all. Do you hear me? Not at all. And you never saw Danton, either.'

'He wasn't here.'

'That's right, he wasn't. You were upstairs in your room, and you heard your stepmother scream, and when you looked out the window of your room, you saw him, the madman, your former husband, running away. Everyone will believe us. He was on his way here. We've got his letter stating that. And it's what a madman would do, isn't it? Attack someone and then run away."

'Yes, yes,' Dee cried, giving a little laugh. 'It was Gavin. The madman. I looked out the window of my bedroom when I heard Lois cry out, and I saw him running down the driveway.'

'It was your ex-husband.' Mrs. Ricketts

continued to prompt her. She had long since realized that if you wanted Dee to remember anything, it was important to repeat it often.

'Gavin. Yes, it was Gavin,' Dee parroted.

Which meant that she had learned her lines well enough to repeat them when needed. 'You come with me, sweetheart,' Ricketts said, standing. She put a protective arm about Dee's shoulders. 'We need to get you cleaned up before anyone sees you. You must have a shower, and I'll deal with these clothes. There's blood on them, too. I think they'll go in the incinerator.'

'It was him. I recognized him,' Dee said breathlessly, while letting herself be steered upward. 'I didn't do it.'

'Of course you didn't,' Ricketts agreed. 'Just remember what I said, that you saw your ex-husband running away. He is a madman, isn't he? People will believe that's what a madman would do. Just you tell them what I said. Can you remember everything?'

'I'll remember,' Dee said.

What Ricketts was already thinking, but did not say aloud, not wanting to worry her little girl, was that this story would hold water only so long as Lois remained unconscious. As soon as she recovered, the truth would surely come out.

If Lois ever recovered.

★ ★ ★

'So, tell me again,' Jake Jango said, 'who exactly are these Carters?'

'Oh, they are, they are sort of my family,' Helen Feather said. 'Let me think. Aunt Paula was my father's sister, as I recall.'

'As you recall? You don't know for certain if they were related or not?'

'Well, they weren't close. They hadn't been for years. I think they'd had no contact for years and years. But, yes, she was his sister. And she married Douglas Carter. Uncle Doug. Rich Uncle Doug.'

'Okay, so your aunt and uncle, then,' Jake said. 'Which does mean family, and not sort of, either.'

'Yes. Only, it's not quite that simple. Aunt Paula is gone now. She passed, oh, it's surely been ten years ago.'

'So then they're not really your family, is what you're saying. These Carters we're on our way to visit.'

'Uncle Doug is still around though. And still rich, I guess, though probably not so much so as we thought of him then.'

'What way is he rich? Just out of curiosity.'

'Oh, from construction stuff, I think. Strip malls, if memory serves. But he was never real bright, either. I think it was mostly nothing more than lucky timing. Strip malls were just beginning to take hold in Los Angeles back then, part of the car thing. A lot of people made fortunes from them without even trying. I think that's how it was with Uncle Doug. It sort of fell into his lap. He just plain got lucky.'

'Well, then, the way I see it, these people are not really related to you, are they? I mean, this Doug person, he was your late aunt's husband, but she's dead. So he's not really blood relation, is he?

Which means the rest of them aren't either.'

'Except, there is Dee. And Annie, too, of course.'

'Who are?'

'Their daughters, Uncle Doug and Aunt Paula's girls. My cousins, if I've got it right. That wouldn't have changed when Aunt Paula passed, I don't think. So they are still family, at least.'

'And this Doug person? Uncle Doug? But he's really not, is he? Your uncle, I mean?'

'Well, I still call him that: my Uncle. He's always been Uncle Doug. And his wife, I mean his second wife, I have always called her Aunt Lois, though I guess technically she is not related at all. And then there's Grace. She is Uncle Doug's mother, so I guess that makes her the family matriarch. And she must be, oh, Lordy, let me think, she must be eighty something by now. Maybe ninety.'

'If she's still even around, you mean.'

'She must be. I think for sure they would have let me know if she had kicked the bucket. Besides, the old girl is too damned stubborn to go without a struggle. She can be pretty contrary if she puts her mind to it.'

'I know the type.' Jake laughed. 'And you used to live with these people?'

'I did, but only for four months, not even quite that. My mom was dead, in a car crash, and then when my dad had to go into the nursing home, I was only seventeen, and the state wouldn't let me live on my own. So then I remembered Aunt Paula. But that was only until I was eighteen. As soon as I could I hightailed it out of there. And I've only been back once, briefly. For Aunt Paula's funeral. That's when I met Lois, but she wasn't married to Uncle Doug then, though I felt pretty sure they were already sleeping together. They got married later, and they sent me an invitation, but I didn't go. By that time, I'd had enough of the Carters.'

'Okay, but here's what I don't understand. If you didn't like living there then, which it sounds like you didn't, why are we going there now?'

'It's just a family visit,' Helen said. 'Well, I guess if I'm going to be honest, then I'm going there because I want to show them.'

'Show them what, for Pete's sake?'

Just . . . '' Helen struggled for the words. 'Just show them, is all. I was like, oh, I don't know, I was just the poor relation to the Carters.'

'Are you saying they were mean to you?'

'No, not exactly. Well, yes, Dee was. Dee was a bitch, no two ways about it. Dee was meanness on the hoof. Annie was nice, just kind of vague. But the rest of the family? If anything, they hardly seemed to notice I was there. Which, when you are a kid, when you really *are* the poor relation, it hurts. So I guess I would say that most of them were mean by omission.'

'Then why are we going there now?' Jake asked.

Helen had to think about that for a minute. 'I think it's because I want them to see me, who I am,' she said. 'I want them to see that I turned out all right, which I don't think anyone expected. I think they thought I'd end up on skid row or something. You know, sleeping in doorways, a bottle of cheap wine in a paper bag. And I guess because I want to see them, too. I am curious to know if those impressions I have carried with me all these years are even true. Maybe they were not all of them as self-absorbed as I thought them then. Maybe Uncle Doug wasn't really the big stupid bag of wind that I thought he was. Maybe, just maybe, Dee wasn't really a bitch. Ha ha, I'm just kidding about that one. You know, I had never actually thought of it before, but maybe she is the real reason I want to go visit. Maybe for once I can show her up, the way she always showed me up in the past.'

'If I'm hearing you rightly, then, you're saying we are going to spend a week of our vacation in Burbank, just so you can get revenge? Is that what this trip boils down to?'

'It does sound silly, doesn't it? When you put it like that.' Helen thought for a moment. 'I don't really know. All I do know is that this is something I have wanted to do for years. Maybe it's even something that I have to do. Does that make any sense?'

Helen caught her breath suddenly. 'Wait, that guy up ahead . . . '

'The one walking alongside the street, in the gutter? What about him?' Jake slowed without stopping as they passed by the man with a duffel bag in one hand, trudging dutifully along by the side of the street. Walking with a pronounced limp. Helen swiveled in her seat to see him from the front.

'I think I know him,' she said. 'Jake, stop the truck. I'll bet he's going to the very same place we are. If he is, we can give him a lift.'

'Why would he be going there? Who is he, anyway?' Jake asked, but he stopped obediently, pulling over next to the curb a few yards past the walking man.

'I think . . . ' Helen stared and shook her head. 'I think it's Gavin Rand.'

'Who is Gavin Rand?'

'Cousin Dee's first husband. As I recall, it was a messy divorce, too.'

'So why would he be going there now? For old time's sake?'

Helen said. 'I have no idea, to be honest. The last I heard, he was in a mental hospital. In Santa Monica.'

'A mental hospital? You want to give a lift to a loony? You know what, Helen, I think you're the loony one.'

Helen ignored that. 'Hi,' she yelled, rolling down her window and sticking her head out. 'Aren't you Gavin?'

The stranger stopped a few feet behind the pickup. 'I am,' he said, suspicious. He coughed, hard. 'Why do you ask that?'

'Are you on your way to the Carter's?' Helen persisted.

The stranger nodded, looking about as if what he really wanted to do was run. He coughed again. 'I am. Yes.'

'Great. That's where we're headed too. Come on, hop in. We'll give you a lift.' Helen scooted over to make room, and whispered hurriedly to Jake, 'I'll explain everything later.'

The man behind the pickup hesitated, looking around as if he was seriously contemplating making a run for it. Finally, with a defeated look, he walked to the door Helen had opened and climbed up into the truck, tossing his duffel bag on the floor at their feet.

'Hi,' Helen said, extending a hand. 'I'm Helen Feather, Aunt Paula's niece. You probably don't even remember me. I was just a kid. You were married to Dee at the time.'

'I sort of remember,' Gavin said. 'But you're right, you were just a teenager as I recall. I think the family must have been a little embarrassed by you. They sort of kept you, I don't know, off by yourself.'

'That they did,' Helen said with a bitter kind of chuckle. 'I think they were embarrassed. The poor relation and all. This, by the way, driving the truck, is my friend, Jake Jango.'

Jake reached around Helen to offer a hand. 'Wow, you feel hot. Do you have a fever?'

'I . . . I don't know. Do I?' Gavin put a hand over his mouth and coughed.

Helen felt his forehead. 'Oh, crap, you do. You're burning up. Have you been walking a long time?'

'I started out yesterday, from Santa Monica.'

'That's a long hike. And you've still got a ways to go. Didn't you even think about taking a bus?'

'In Los Angeles?' Gavin said. 'Anyway, it wasn't like I said, right off the bat, I'm going to walk to Burbank. I just started out walking. And then, after a while, I did decide, you know what, I can do this, and, well, here I am. But to tell the truth, I believe I've got a bad foot.'

'You believe?' Jake said.

Gavin made a motion with his shoulders that might have been a shrug, but that came out more like a nervous spasm. 'I thought for a while it was psychosomatic, but it really does seem to be bad. I broke it, a long time ago, actually, but it seems not to have healed properly. I thought it was okay, but it was starting to give me some trouble as I walked. Especially today. So I'd have had to quit before long anyway, probably.'

Jake carefully entered the traffic on the street again. Helen looked at Gavin thoughtfully, and again put a hand to his forehead. 'I don't know, the fever, and that cough. Maybe instead of the Carters we should take you to a hospital, or something like that.'

'No,' Gavin said sharply, and then, more pacifically, 'No, I just want to see the family. Well, to see Dee, actually. I have to discuss something with her. Then I'll go. If it's a problem, I mean, I can walk, or, or something. Maybe those buses, like you said. If you see a bus stop you can just drop me off.'

'No, it's not a problem,' Helen said, 'absolutely not. No bus stops. We'll take you.'

'So, Gavin,' Jake said, speaking carefully, 'Helen says you were in a hospital.'

'You don't have to pick your words,' Gavin said sharply. 'What you mean is, I was in a mental hospital. Fruitcake city. And the answer is, yes, I was.'

'Please tell me you're not an escapee,' Jake said with a laugh, but his expression was dead serious. 'You're not on the run, are you?'

Gavin sighed. 'No, I'm not on the run, as you put it. Actually, if you want to know, I was discharged nearly a year ago.'

'But you're just now going home?' Jake

asked. 'After a year's wait?'

'To be perfectly honest, I never exactly thought of it as going home,' Gavin said. 'The Carter's house was never really home to me. I just married one of the daughters.'

'You didn't come from here, did you?' Helen asked. 'Los Angeles, I mean?'

'No. Kansas. A little town near Topeka.'

'How did you get from Kansas to L.A.?' Jake asked.

'Marine Corps,' Gavin said. 'I enlisted. They sent me to Pendleton. It's just down the road.'

'And somehow your path here crossed with that of Dee Carter,' Helen said.

'I met her in a bar. In Hollywood.' Gavin sighed. 'Next thing I knew, we were married.'

'And you were one of the Carters.'

Gavin sighed. 'I was in such awe of that family, the Carters. They seemed like, some, I don't know exactly what. Like some kind of American dream.'

'Which still leaves that odd time gap, that year,' Jake said. 'If you don't mind my harping on it.'

'Oh, that. If you really want to know the reason for the delay, I was helping my doctor at the hospital, Doctor Dawes. As a sort of a voluntary assistant.'

'Meaning no pay?' Helen said.

Gavin continued to cough. 'Right. See, he was my therapist for a long time and he was very kind to me. I wanted to repay him, and that was the only way I knew how. Plus, I'd sort of been thinking about doing the same kind of work, so it was a chance to try it out. Like get my feet wet.'

'Your feet look like they could use a good soak,' Helen said. 'And I don't like the sound of that cough. Turn left at the next light, Jake.'

'Did you say exactly why you're visiting the family?' Jake asked, making the turn. They were on a residential street now. Del Mar Lane, a sign said.

'I . . . we, Dee and me, we had a baby. A little boy. I wanted to find out how the baby was doing.'

'That makes sense,' Helen said. 'Only of course he isn't a baby by now.'

'Yes. Which is why this visit.'

Del Mar Lane meandered through

groves of oak and eucalyptus. The sunshine was dappled, the air smelled of lavender. Bees droned in the geraniums growing alongside the quiet street. Just ahead, the street formed a V.

'Go right, up the hill,' Helen instructed Jake. 'It's the third driveway on the left, the one with the wrought iron gates.'

'Will we be able to get in?' Jake asked.

'No problem. They're always open.'

'Very welcoming, I'd say,' Jake said, driving toward the open gates.

'Welcoming?' Gavin asked.

'Open gates,' Jake said. 'It's like a gesture of welcome, isn't it? It sort of says, come on in.'

'Trust me. It's an illusion,' Gavin said. 'That welcome invitation.'

'You sound nervous. Are you afraid, Gavin?' Helen asked.

'Of seeing Dee again? Of course I am.'

'Me too, I guess.' What Helen didn't say is that she had faced fear often; often enough to have come to think that maybe fear was necessary in some way, that it gave life some needed flavor, like salting your soup. An existence that was always safe, cozy, free from danger, would be awfully boring, wouldn't it?

And maybe, she thought, that had something to do with her determination to make this visit just at the present. Maybe wanting vengeance was an essential part of living, Biblical proscriptions notwithstanding. After all, if no one was hankering for it, why would it even be worth mentioning?

'But, when it comes to facing Dee,' Gavin said, 'in my case, it has to be done. Sooner or later it's going to happen. Just as well to get it out of the way now. Besides, as I said, I want to talk with her about our boy. Plus, I have my own reasons for wanting to do it now, without any delays.'

They were passing through the open gates when Gavin suddenly said, out of the blue, 'Can we stop here for a second, please?'

'Here?' Jake asked, but he stopped. To his surprise and Helen's, Gavin lowered his window and gave his duffel bag a toss, landing it in the bushes just beyond the gate.

'I hadn't planned on staying for more than a few minutes. Just long enough to talk to Dee about my son,' he said in way of explanation as he put the window back up. 'If I carry that thing inside, someone will get the wrong idea. This way, I can just stop and pick it up on the way out. Makes everything mellower.'

The asphalt drive curved its graceful way through a wide front lawn and brought them to a wider gravel-covered space, obviously a parking area. In its center a fountain shot a column of water into the air. On the other side of the fountain, stone steps led up to a red painted door and beyond the graveled area, the drive disappeared around the house to the rear, presumably to the garages.

'Shoot,' Helen said, making a moue of disappointment. 'You'd sort of expect a porte cochère, wouldn't you?'

'It's a nice house, though,' Jake said, parking on the gravel and cutting the engine. It continued to make ticking noises while they sat and looked. 'Anyway, you already knew there wasn't one, didn't you?'

'Just cracking wise,' Helen said. 'But

39

you're right, it is nice. I always thought so.'

It was indeed a pleasant looking domicile, white except for that door, like a bloody gash in the surrounding starkness. The house was larger than its neighbors, though not greatly so, and it said 'money,' but in a muted murmur and the gentle plash of water rather than a shout. A jacaranda tree, now in full bloom, shaded the big multi-paned bay window to the right of the door, and shrubs cut lower stood below the bay window on the left.

For a long moment no one in the truck moved. The engine continued to ping on a diminuendo. All three of them sat and stared at that red door, as if it might suddenly burst open to welcome them inside. It stayed obstinately closed, however.

'It looks like no one's here,' Jake said, frowning.

'That's odd. They knew I was coming,' Helen said. 'I sent a letter.'

'Me too. I wrote Dee a letter, anyway,' Gavin said. 'Days ago. From Santa Monica. She must have gotten it by now.'

He tried to get out of the truck, but when he put his feet down on the ground, his legs gave out on him and he would have fallen if he had not been holding on to the door.

'Oh, wait, let me help you,' Helen cried, jumping out past him. 'Jake, give us a hand, please.'

Jake got quickly out his side and came around the truck and took hold of Gavin's other arm.

The two of them supporting Gavin on either side, they made their way up the steps to the red door, where Helen got a hand free to ring the bell.

It was so long before it was answered that they had begun to think there was no one at home after all.

'They must have got my letter,' Helen said. 'I mailed it a week ago.'

'Maybe not,' Jake said, but the door swung inward just at that moment to reveal a short young woman inside. A young woman, not fat, certainly, nor even plump, but what anyone might forgivably call well-padded. She wore plain jeans and a white, Mexican-looking tunic, and open-toed leather sandals on her feet. Her hair, thick and glossy and fawn brown, was pulled back from her face with a bright yellow ribbon and her eyes, a darker brown than her hair, were wide just now with evident astonishment.

She stared at the trio on the steps, mouth agape. Her expression was a mix of fatigue, curiosity, and worry — more of the last one than the other two.

'You?' she said directly to Gavin. 'Good grief! You've come back to the scene of the crime?'

3

'Hello, Annie,' Helen said, waving her free hand. 'Remember me? Cousin Helen? And this is my friend, Jake. The big guy. I don't think you've met him.'

'Helen, hi, yes of course I remember you,' she said, grinning. 'And hi to you too, Mr. Big Guy.'

'Jake,' he said. 'Jake Jango.'

'Jake, then.' She held out a hand to Jake, and he took it.

'Annie's a cousin too,' Helen said. 'Dee's sister.'

'And the family's ugly duckling, in case you hadn't figured that out,' Annie said.

'That sounds suspiciously like Dee talk,' Helen said.

'I'm just saying what everyone thinks,' Annie said defensively.

'Not everyone,' Helen said.

'Name one who doesn't,' she said.

'In this family? Well, me for one.' Helen shrugged.

'Aw, shucks,' she said, and made a kind of goofy curtsy.

'Besides, I thought you were away,' Helen said.

'I was. I was away at school. Way back east. As far away as I could go, frankly. But I just came home for break. I'm not even sure why. I don't think anybody cared. I doubt if they even noticed I'm here, to be honest.'

'Uh, hello, Annie,' Gavin said, intruding on their chat. 'Speaking of noticing. In case you didn't notice me.'

'I did notice you, Gavin, I surely did,' she said, giving him a solemn look. 'But, Gavin, the rest of the family will be back any minute now. To tell the truth, I'm only here because I remembered that Helen was coming today, which everybody else seemed to have forgotten,' she said. 'So I begged off going with them. Anyway, hospitals are not my thing.'

'Thanks for remembering me,' Helen said. 'I should have realized they would all forget.'

'You're welcome. And I suppose you could cut them some slack, under the circumstances. But if they find him here,' she nodded toward Gavin, 'all hell is likely to break loose. Helen, you have to get him out of here. Right now.'

'We can't,' Helen said. 'For starters, the man is sick. He's burning up with a fever. Feel his forehead if you don't believe me.' Gavin coughed accommodatingly.

'Then take him to a hospital,' Annie said without checking Gavin's forehead. 'Or I don't know where, just take him. Away. Anywhere but here.'

'Don't talk like that. You sound like Dee. Is there a room ready for me?' Helen asked.

'Of course there is, your old room. I just finished making the bed myself. But I don't think you should try to . . . '

'My old room? Then that's where we're taking him. And never mind showing us where it is, I know the way,' Helen said, and to Jake, 'It's all the way to the back, through the kitchen. The worst room in the place, just an add-on, an afterthought. Like me, I suppose. Come on, team, this way.'

From the door and the wood-tiled

foyer, three steps led down into the richly carpeted living room, two stories high, with stairs to their right that led up to a landing and a gallery that ran the length of the house and off of which a series of doors, all of them now closed, led. Sunlight spilled down from a skylight above. On the left, a massive floral arrangement sat atop an antique-ish looking credenza. A tall grandfather clock stood against a nearby wall.

With Annie trailing behind them and Jake helping him hold Gavin erect, Helen steered them down the steps from the foyer, through the front room, which despite the lack of air conditioning and the sunlight was pleasantly cool after the heat outside.

Jake, hurrying along, had no more than glimpses of the front room: A large room, mostly dark now, filled almost to the point of clutter with big, slipcovered sofas and chairs, beautiful wood pieces, taste and money coming together, as it often did not, in a harmonious blend. The grandfather clock gave a sort of wheeze of its innards, as if clearing its throat, and began to chime the hour, sounding arrogantly loud in the house's stillness.

From the front room they passed through a swinging door into the kitchen, then a pantry and the landing of a stairwell that led cellar-wise downward, all the way to a room at the very rear of the house.

'If we went any further,' Helen said with a laugh when they got there, 'we'd be in the next door neighbor's yard. Which you can see from the window. Uh, there's just the one window, by the way.'

The room clearly was, as Helen had said, an add-on, and with cardboard boxes stacked against one wall, it looked more like a storage room than an actual bedroom, notwithstanding the queen-sized bed that occupied much of the small space. The room had been left somewhat unfinished, too. The ceiling was still open to reveal the metal beams that would otherwise be covered. The whole space had a temporary, nobody-really-cares look.

'Sorry about the boxes,' Annie said. 'I couldn't find anywhere else to put them so I just piled them there for the time being. Maybe the cellar, if someone can help me carry them? The family has been using this space for temporary storage.'

'Which I guess you could say is what it always was,' Helen said. 'You've dusted, at least.'

Annie shook her head. 'Didn't need to. The furniture was all covered with muslin. I told you this room has only been used for storage, but the furnishings stayed in it. Probably because they had no place else to put them.'

Helen bobbed her chin in Gavin's direction. 'Here, let's put him down on the bed.' They dropped Gavin rather unceremoniously on the surface of the bed.

'Ooof,' Gavin grunted and struggled to sit back up.

'Never mind trying to get up,' Helen said. 'Just lie right there. I'll see if I can find you some aspirin and a glass of water. I won't be a minute.'

'My shoes,' Gavin said, wriggling his feet. 'They're killing my feet. Can someone help me get them off? Please.'

Jake looked around the room and decided Helen was right. Compared to what he had seen of the rest of the house, this room was pretty crappy. Habitable, but only just.

'You lie still. I'll get them,' Jake said and knelt down to deal with the shoes. When he took them off, he discovered that Gavin's right foot was purplish and swollen. 'That one looks nasty,' Jake said, standing.

'I told you before, I broke it a while back,' Gavin mumbled. 'I thought it would be okay, but I don't think all that walking on it was a good idea.'

'Probably not,' Jake agreed. 'It looks pretty wicked.'

Helen had hurried to the somewhat primitive bathroom off the sleeping area. She came back with a jelly glass full of water. 'No aspirin in there, but I think I've got some in my bag.' She handed Annie the jelly glass. 'Here, take this. I'll be back in a jiff.'

She disappeared at a run and was back in astonishingly few minutes carrying her suitcase and Jake's. She set them on the

49

floor and opening hers, rooted around in it. 'Ah, here they are. I knew I had them with me,' she said, standing with a bottle in her hand. She uncapped it and rolled two aspirin onto her palm and snatched the glass of water back from Annie.

'Here you go,' she said, helping Gavin to sit up long enough to swallow the pills and a big swig of water, after which Gavin plopped back down again on the bed with a loud groan.

'Thanks,' he murmured. 'Man. Am I beat.'

'Did you hear me, Helen?' Jake asked. 'About his foot. It looks bad. He wasn't kidding about that.'

'Helen,' Annie said, 'I wasn't kidding about the family either. They're due back any minute now.'

'You said that before. Back from where, did you say?' Helen asked.

'They're all at the hospital.'

'Ah yes, you did tell us that's where they were,' Helen said, nodding. 'But I don't think you told us what they are there for. Is someone sick?'

'Lois is in a coma,' she said. 'That's my

stepmother, Jake. They all went to see her. Everyone except me. It was sort of like a pilgrimage.'

'What?' Helen was aghast. 'Aunt Lois? In a coma? How did that happen? Was that what you meant, about the scene of the crime?'

She turned her eyes toward the man on the bed. 'Maybe you should ask him,' she said.

'I don't know anything about it,' Gavin said weakly. He lifted a hand to wipe some spit from around his mouth. 'How could I? I just got here, you know.'

'Are you trying to say you weren't here last night?' she demanded.

Gavin raised his head from the pillow. 'Here? In this house, you mean? Last night? I slept in someone's back yard last night,' he said. 'On a cushion I took off a chaise longue. This was somewhere in West Hollywood, I think. I climbed a fence.'

'But he . . . ' Annie sputtered. 'He was here. Dee said he was, she said she saw him, running away, down the drive, afterwards.'

51

'After what?' Helen asked.

'Well, after he attacked Lois, is what. That's why she is in the hospital, in a coma.'

'Well, if what Dee says is so, he must have run quite a distance,' Helen said. 'We picked him up along the street; it must have been fifteen miles from here, and not more than half an hour ago. Calm yourself down, Annie, and just tell us what is supposed to have happened.'

'Dee says,' she paused to take a deep breath and started again. 'She says he came here last night. He wanted to know about the baby, it seems.'

'That part of it is true enough,' Gavin said. 'That *is* why I came, to find out about the baby. I wrote Dee a letter, to tell her that. I wanted to have a discussion about him.'

'But didn't you know?' Annie asked him. 'Your boy, Lennie, is . . . well, he's retarded. Autistic to be politically correct. He was born that way.'

'No, I didn't know that,' Gavin said. 'I was, you know, they sent me away, before she had the baby. Someone wrote me to say that she'd had a boy. That's as much as I knew.'

'That was me,' Annie said. 'I'm the one who wrote you. I thought you had a right to know. But I didn't say anything about the autism in my letter.'

'There's different kinds. Or maybe I mean different degrees,' Helen said. 'So, when you say autistic . . . ?'

'As I understand it,' Annie said, 'he can't, well, he doesn't talk right, apparently. Or think right, for that matter. I don't mean to say — he's not an imbecile, but he is slow. At least that's what I was told.'

She turned to Gavin. 'I don't really even know now why I thought it would be better if you didn't know that. It was just your being where you were and all. It wasn't like there was anything you could do about it.'

'Probably not,' Gavin said. 'No, you're right, of course you are. There was nothing I could do. But what did *they* do? Dee, I mean, and the family?'

'They sent him to a home up north, in Monterey, a place where they specialize in kids with disabilities. Right after he was born. Not exactly right after, but as soon as they knew about, oh, you know, his problem. So maybe he was one year old or two.'

'What home?' Gavin demanded, sitting full up.

The question surprised her. 'I . . . I don't actually know the name of the place. It's in Monterey, is all I know. Like I said, they sent him there when he was just a baby. That must be, gosh, two or three years ago.'

'I need to find out,' Gavin said, looking at Helen. 'He's my kid too. If she doesn't want him then I do. I don't care about the mental stuff. I just want him to have a home, a real home. With someone who cares about him.'

'Whoa, slow down a minute,' Helen said. 'First off, are you even qualified to care for a small child?'

'I'm not, no. But I had someone else in mind who is.'

'Besides,' Helen added, 'I don't know what kind of claim you even have. After the last time you were here.'

'Not to mention this time,' Annie said darkly.

'Okay,' Jake said. 'What exactly did happen?'

'The last time? When they sent him away?' Helen asked. 'Dee says he attacked her.'

'I didn't. I have no idea why she even said that.' Gavin said, falling back on the bed.

'Humm,' Helen grunted. 'I could probably give you a reason or two.'

'And this time?' Jake said.

'I told you about this time,' Annie cried, exasperated. 'Lois was attacked. Last night. And now she's in the hospital, in a coma.'

'Attacked where?' Helen asked. 'How?'

'Right here. Well, not in this room. In the front room, I mean. She was apparently alone in the front of the house. Mrs. Ricketts, that's the maid,' she said in a fast aside to Jake, 'she was in the kitchen, and Dee was upstairs, so nobody actually saw what happened. Mrs. Ricketts said she thought she heard the doorbell, but her hearing supposedly isn't

55

very good. Anyway, then she says she heard Lois talking to someone,'

'She was probably listening at the door,' Helen said.

'Probably, knowing Ricketts,' Annie agreed with a titter. 'It's the kind of thing she does. So, anyway, she says she heard conversation, not loud enough to hear what was being said, just the sound of voices, and she says she thought that if there had been someone at the door, Lois must have let whoever it was in, so Ricketts figured she wasn't needed and she went back to whatever she was cooking. Then the next thing she heard was Lois gave a yell, and when Ricketts ran into the front room she found Lois on the floor, all bloody and already unconscious. And Dee said when she heard our stepmother yell, she looked out the window of her bedroom and saw Gavin, running away.'

'Sounds like a kind of odd reaction to me,' Jake said. 'Going to her window to look out. I'd think the first thing you would do is, you'd want to see what the yell was all about, wouldn't you?'

'I would, for sure. Dee's bedroom,

that's upstairs, still?' Helen asked.

'Right. First door, top of the stairs. And she saw him.' She jerked her thumb in Gavin's direction. 'She said he was running away, down the driveway, toward the street. And Aunt Lois never did wake up. Like I said, she's been in a coma since. At Meredith General. And that's where everybody is. But they're due back any minute now. They left hours ago. I happen to know that visiting hours end at ten there, and it's after eleven now, so even if they stopped for coffee or some-thing, which they must have, they'll be pulling in any second now.'

Annie held her lips pressed tightly together, face tensed, as if determined not to cry.

'But it wasn't me, I tell you,' Gavin said in a plaintive voice. 'I just got here.'

'That's true. Annie, think,' Helen said. 'He couldn't have been here and gotten to where we picked him up. And you can see for yourself he's sick. He couldn't have run down the drive. He couldn't have run anywhere probably. As far as that goes, I doubt he could have attacked anybody either. He's as weak as a kitten. You saw us, we had to help him inside. He couldn't even walk. If he attacked Lois, I would think he would be the one in a coma.'

'Well . . . ' Annie screwed up her face in thought. 'Okay, you probably are right. What you say makes sense. But it isn't going to make any difference to them. They're all convinced. They think he did it. They're saying he escaped somehow from that loony bin.'

Gavin groaned aloud again but she ignored him. 'They say he came here to have it out with Dee about the baby,'

'I did, that is why I came,' Gavin said, but she ignored the interruption and went on with what she had been saying.

'But Lois answered the door and when he insisted upon seeing Dee, she must have tried to head him off, and apparently he attacked her. And like I told you, Dee said she saw him, running off. Plus, Dad — that's Doug, Jake — if Helen hasn't told you, he has a gun. He says if he even sets eyes on Gavin, he's going to shoot first and ask questions later.'

'He's not the most rational man in the world,' Helen said. 'Hot-headed, for sure.'

'So what are we going to do?' Annie asked. 'If Gavin stays here, he's a goner, that's for sure.'

'Dee says she saw him running down the driveway?' Jake said. 'That driveway out front? The one we just drove up?'

'I guess so. It's the only driveway up to the house, so, yes, that's the one,' Annie said, hesitantly. 'Why?'

'I'm just wondering. This was at night, right? After dark?'

'Yes, it was, like maybe nine o'clock, nine thirty, I believe. I had gone out with some friends. They dropped me off about ten and apparently it had happened not long before. So, say nine thirty.'

'Is the front yard floodlit at night?'

'No. There's just a porch light at the front door. Enough to light up the front steps. The rest of the grounds are dark by that time of night, even in summer.'

'So, Dee was in her bedroom, upstairs you said, which puts it maybe forty, fifty feet away, looking down at a dark drive-way, and a man running away with his back to her, and she says she can identify him?'

'When you put it like that,' Annie said, looking puzzled, 'it does seem unlikely.'

'She must have been mistaken,' Gavin said.

'What seems more likely to me,' Helen said, 'is that Dee is lying.' She gave Annie a significant look. 'Annie, you know as well as I do, it would not be the first time she told people fibs.'

Annie sighed. 'No, you're probably right about that too. My sister is a liar. We both know that. But that still leaves us with the same question: what are we going to do about him?' She again jerked her thumb in the direction of the bed, where Gavin now appeared to be drifting off to sleep. He coughed again, but without opening his eyes. His chest had begun to rise and fall rhythmically.

'In the first place,' Helen said, 'it looks to me like he's falling asleep. And we're going to let him sleep if he can. I think he seriously needs it. Even when they get home, no one is likely to come back here, so they won't see him. They don't even

60

need to know he's here, do they?' He gave Annie a challenging look.

'If Ricketts is in the kitchen, she might hear him,' Annie said, ignoring the challenge. 'If he snores, or say he coughs. He has been coughing a lot since you brought him in.'

'He has,' Jake said. 'But this Ricketts person, where is she now?'

'She asked if she could go with the family to the hospital,' Annie said, and screwed up her face thoughtfully. 'Which, when you think of it, is odd in itself. She and Lois were never really close, so far as I could say. I wonder why she wanted to go? I guess just because everyone else was going.'

'If Ricketts is as devoted to Dee as you say,' Helen said, 'she was probably up to something. Or the two of them are. That sounds like the real explanation to me.'

'She's the maid, you said?' Jake asked. 'This Ricketts?'

'Yes' Annie said. 'Well, housekeeper, I guess you'd say. And also Dee's slave. Dee's always had Ricketts twisted about her little finger. Since she was a child.

They've had a kind of unholy alliance, from the day Ricketts first came here.'

'Which was after my time,' Helen said. 'I only met her once, on that visit when your Mom passed away.'

'And didn't you say she was hard of hearing?' Jake asked. 'This Ricketts?'

'She is,' Annie said. 'Or at least she claims to be, but I've never been entirely convinced. And she is a bit slow, too, but don't quote me. I said that once and Dee like to took my head off.'

'And there's the pantry and the cellar stairs between here and the kitchen,' Helen said. 'If she really is hard of hearing, Gavin would have to bang on a drum for her to know he was here.'

'Okay, that's probably so,' Annie said. 'Even if she's not, she still isn't likely to hear him, I guess.'

She laughed, for the first time since they had been there, and it was as if a phoenix had suddenly popped up from a pile of ashes. Her laughter was a lovely sound, soft and melodious, and it transformed her: Her dark eyes sparkled, and dimples appeared at the corners of her mouth. She was still short and well padded, and suddenly surprisingly attractive as well.

Jake, staring, thought, 'But she's pretty. Who told her she was an ugly duckling?' And Helen thought, 'I always knew she was brighter than Dee, but she's prettier too. I'll bet no one has ever told her that.'

And she was pretty. Despite her ample curves, her face was small and narrow, framed by a halo of light brown hair. Her complexion was as smooth as porcelain, the kind that did not need to be disguised by makeup — which was just as well, as she rarely wore any. Her eyes were clear and liquid, her lashes naturally long and thick.

Completely unaware of what the two were thinking, Annie, grew serious again, but there remained in her throat the last sweet taste of laughter, and so she remained prettier than she had ever been before, perhaps never again to be the ugly duckling she had always seen herself as being.

She said, into the silence that had fallen over them, over the room, 'But what are you planning? You're going to leave him here for how long? Obviously he can't stay forever. You're right, they aren't likely to come back here, not right away, at least, but sooner or later, they are going to find out he's here. That's inevitable, seems to me. And like I said, Dad's got a gun.'

'And Doug's dumb enough to use it,' Helen said. 'Sorry, Annie, I know he's your father.'

'That's okay. And you're right. I love him, but he's not the brightest.' And she laughed again, which again enchanted both of them.

'And yes, sooner or later,' Helen said, 'I am going to have to tell them about him, and that he's here. I just have to think how, and who I'm going to tell. Not Doug, I don't think. He loves Dee. He'll believe whatever she tells him. The same as Ricketts, if what you say is true. And Aunt Lois is obviously out. Who does that leave?'

'Granny?' Annie said hesitantly.

'Hmm. Maybe. I'll have to think about that.'

'In the meantime,' Jake said, 'He told

us, Gavin did, that he had not escaped from that mental hospital. He says he was properly discharged. And he told us his doctor's name. Dawes, wasn't it Helen?' Helen nodded. 'I think before you tell the family the guy is here, maybe we ought to visit that doctor. If he says the dude is okay, that ought to calm everyone down a bit.'

'If Dad hasn't already shot him,' Annie said.

'Which, knowing Doug, is entirely possible,' Helen agreed.

'In the meantime,' Jake said, 'I think Helen is right. Gavin needs to sleep. It's not just that foot. I think he really is sick. Seriously sick. That cough, and his physical weakness. They don't seem so good.'

'So, Annie,' Helen said, 'We just need you to keep quiet about him.'

'I'll do whatever you say, of course, you know that, Helen,' she said. 'To be honest, I thought when Dee was telling everybody her story she sounded a little too, well, you know how she is, Helen.'

'Exactly,' Helen said. 'A little too.'

'But they all believed her?' Jake said.

Helen sighed. 'They always believe her.'

'That's true,' Annie said, sighing as well. 'Do you remember that time with the parakeet, Helen? Our mother had this bird, a little yellow parakeet, named Gwenevere,' she told Jake. 'She loved that little thing, and she kept him in a cage in the den, so the cat couldn't get at him. Only, one day, the door to her cage was left open, and the bird got out, and the cat got him. There was nothing left but a scattering of yellow feathers on the carpet.'

'Dee was in the den earlier that day, playing with the bird. She had the parakeet out of the cage,' Helen said. 'We both saw her.'

'I know that, and you know that, but Dee swore she wasn't even in the room that day.'

'So,' Helen said, 'it came down to Annie or me. Dee said it must have been one of us who left the cage door open. And since neither of us would con-fess . . . '

'How could we?' Annie said hotly. 'Why

should we? We hadn't either of us done anything to confess.'

'But we both got punished,' Helen finished the story.

'We were grounded,' Annie said. 'For two weeks. No books, no TV, no desserts. Dee even got my ice cream, in fact. She got two servings.'

'Plus, they took the radio out of my room,' Helen said.

'And this is the one who might get him killed?' Jake nodded his head in the direction of the man, now sound asleep, lying on the bed. 'Dee?'

'She could,' Helen said. 'And would. Knowing Dee.'

4

'You know, they don't seem all that rich to me,' Jake said. 'The Carters. Middle class, I'd have said. Upper middle class, maybe.'

They were on the freeway. Helen had been playing with the tuning dial on the radio, searching for some background kind of music. She settled for a country western station. Which, as she saw it, qualified for easy listening.

'That's because you've never seen Grannie's jewels,' she said. 'They'd put Tiffany's to shame. She's got a diamond necklace, which of course she never wears anymore, platinum and eighteen-carat gold, with cabochon emeralds and rubies. And there's a ring, with a diamond that would choke a horse. A big horse.'

Helen was silent for a few minutes, thinking about the money tied up in all that jewelry. Why had they been so stingy with her?

But it hadn't really been about money either, if she was to be honest with herself. The truth was, she had been for all intents and purposes a stranger to them when she came here that time, never mind the blood ties. They had taken her in, she had to give them that. They had at least seen that she was housed and fed. Physically fed, anyway, though her soul had remained starved.

But what was the point of dwelling on all that old history? It had been what it had been. Maybe Jake was right. Maybe it was time to let it all go. If she didn't feel all this old resentment toward Dee, things might be entirely different. But there was no use pretending, she did resent her.

'It's strange, isn't it?' she said after they had gone a few miles.

'What's that?' Jake asked, without taking his eyes away from the road ahead.

'I was just thinking.' Satisfied with the station she had found, Helen turned the volume lower and leaned back in her seat. 'It took Gavin Rand two days to walk from Santa Monica to Burbank, and we're going to drive from Burbank to

Santa Monica in forty-five minutes.'

'Thirty minutes,' Jake said.

'Okay, yes, probably thirty minutes, the way you drive.'

'You don't like the way I drive?' Jake asked, surprised.

'I do, only . . . wait, did you just cut off that sweet little old lady in the vintage Plymouth?'

'She had no business driving fifty miles per hour in the fast lane,' Jake said curtly. 'Of course I cut her off. Who wouldn't?'

★   ★   ★

The Plymouth quickly disappeared behind them. Jake was now cruising the freeway at an easy seventy miles per hour. They switched from The Golden State Freeway, with purplish mountains in the far distance, to the Hollywood, dipping down between the high rises of downtown Los Angeles, like descending into a canyon.

The sky as they passed through downtown Los Angeles was sooty colored, but the closer they got to the ocean the bluer it became, like someone had painted it on with a roller. The air was hot. The pavement on the highway ahead of them seemed to shimmer. They had opted for windows partially down rather than the air conditioning, which Helen did not care for, so the heated air from outside blew over them in a continuous drying stream, along with the noise of all the other cars on the freeway with them, continuous streams of vehicles going both directions.

'You know, Helen,' Jake said, all but shouting over the noise from outside, 'when we first met, I have to confess, I didn't much like you. I suppose you felt the same way at the time, huh?'

'I thought you were a jerk,' Helen said.

'Wow! You did?' Jake gave her a surprised glance. 'I was that bad?'

'Well, a jerk with possibilities,' Helen said. 'If that makes you feel better.'

'Huh?' Jake honked at a slow moving station wagon in front of him. The driver glanced at his rear view mirror and raised a hand as if about to give him the finger, but one glimpse of that huge red pickup behind him, or maybe he saw who was driving it, apparently changed his mind.

He moved over to the right, setting off a cacophony of horns. Los Angeles freeway drivers were notoriously territorial.

'I thought you were in love with me,' Jake said, sailing by the station wagon and ignoring the angry scowls of its driver.

'Not at the first I wasn't. That came later. I think. Or, oh, I don't know. It was all kind of confusing, wasn't it? I still don't think I understand how we ended up, well, you know, whatever we are.'

'Partners,' Jake said. 'That's what we are. And, yeah, it is kind of funny when you think about it, isn't it? You and me?'

'Hilarious,' Helen said sarcastically. 'But it has been a couple of years for us now. That's kind of a record. For me, anyway.'

Which, although it was certainly true, was a fact for which Helen as yet had no explanation. She did not feel that when she had met Jake she had been looking for anything like the relationship that had developed between them, although it was indeed true that she had often longed for someone in her life — but had she thought about it, it would almost certainly not have been this particular someone. Or this particular relationship, whatever exactly it might be.

'You know,' she said thoughtfully, 'When you first meet someone, it's the little oddities that endear them to you. The crooked teeth, the eyes that aren't quite aligned. But, later, those are the very same things that drive you up the wall, aren't they? You run into them, a couple of years later, say at a party, and you wonder what the hell you ever saw in them. And it's the funny teeth and the funny eyes that most turn you off.'

'I guess I'm lucky, then,' Jake said. 'I never got turned on to your teeth or your eyes. It was your butt that interested me.'

'Does it still?'

'Do you need to ask?' They both laughed at that.

So how had it happened, Helen wondered? Whatever exactly 'it' was, of which she was still in some confusion. Yes, it had started out the same as they always did: Jake was hot, and macho, super macho. Like catnip, then.

Only, once they had gotten past that

part of it, which is to say, once they had done the bed thing, which for Helen usually meant the interest kind of petered out, Jake had continued to intrigue her, in ways that other guys before him had not.

5

The last time Helen had been at Santa Monica Medical Center it had been at night. Then it had looked like an extravagant wedding cake, white and huge and seemingly iced with rows of brightly shining lights.

In the daytime, it looked much more businesslike. They circled the parking lot twice before they found a space someone was just pulling out of.

By an unspoken agreement, they paused outside the truck. It was almost like catching their breath, as if they had run here instead of driving. After the noise of the freeway the hospital grounds were eerily silent. In the near-distant sky someone was parasailing over the ocean. He seemed to hang suspended against the blue, like an angel. You almost expected him to start singing hosannas. Far above him, so high that it was only a glint of silver, a jet plane sundering the sky left a wake of white trails behind itself.

The sight of the airplane, as it always did, gave Helen a brief pang. She inevitably felt that she should be going somewhere; some distant locale that seemed mysteriously to beckon her. Unfortunately she did not know where it was; but still, it called to her, like Bali Hai in that musical.

'Well,' Jake said, looking away from the man in the sky, 'I guess we need to get to it,' and Helen, resisting the urge to wave goodbye to the plane, said, 'Yes, we might as well go in.'

A large metal can, filled with earth and cigarette butts sprouting like noxious weeds from the glittering sand, stood just outside the main entrance. Inside, the walls were peppered with no smoking signs and the lobby was lined with benches, most of them occupied; mostly, Helen noted, by women and children, the majority of them black or brown. Like survivors in lifeboats, Helen found herself thinking. Probably they had been cast adrift on the stormy seas of physical impairment and insurance coverage. Sink or swim, me hearties.

A severe-looking receptionist behind a wooden counter greeted them as they came into the lobby, and when they told her who they had come to see, she paged Doctor Dawes on a PA system and after a brief telephone conversation, told them he was waiting downstairs for them. She gave them directions for finding the elevator, and after consulting her computer screen, told them his office number.

The psychiatric facilities were below ground. Above, things were decorated nicely with plush sofas and chairs and prints hanging on the wall, all of it brightly lighted; but down here the lighting was dim. At the end of the corridor in which the elevator had deposited them, two dark shadows bickered over space. The furnishings on this level were mostly old and either bare wood or covered in cracked Naugahyde, the prints non-existent. The floors were an ugly brown linoleum and what at first glance appeared to be worn and dark colored carpeting was only more shadow. The walls had long ago been painted a mustardy yellow that had faded to a vomit-like hue. Miles of other corridors branched off in every direction, lined with doors, some of them open, many of them closed.

They passed one of the rooms with an open door and inside they caught a glimpse of a group of people, sitting in a semi-circle on hard-looking wooden chairs and discussing something earnestly, but in low voices. A group session of some sort, Helen thought. She'd been in one or two of those.

Gavin's therapist, Doctor Dawes, was waiting in his own open doorway for them. He turned out to be a short man, no more than five three or four, a bit shy of obesity but stout enough certainly to be flirting with that condition, and with a prominent and jiggly sort of belly. His hair and beard were white, his nose large and red, and his eyes twinkled when he smiled at them. If he'd only had a pipe in his mouth, he'd have looked just like Santa Claus, Helen thought; she half expected to be met with a hearty 'Ho ho ho.'

The doctor's office turned out to be a

pleasant surprise, too, large and, unlike the corridor outside, well-lighted, the walls a welcoming daisy color, the floor carpeted in royal blue. The air conditioning kept everything cool and the air sterile. And, the door closed after them, everything was quiet as well.

'You do realize,' Dawes said when they were all seated about his desk, Jake and Helen to one side, the doctor at the other, 'That I am not free to discuss my patient with you. I wish I could. But no, I cannot, it would violate all kinds of ethics.'

'We do understand that,' Helen said.

'But,' Jake said, 'There are people who think the poor guy escaped from this place. That he's a fugitive, on the run. You can tell us that much, at least, can't you? If he's on the lam or not?'

'Yes, that I can say. Gavin is most certainly not on the run. Not from me, at least. Not from the hospital.'

'But he might be on the run?' Helen said.

'We all might be said to be running from something,' Doctor Dawes said. 'What I meant was, Gavin Rand was discharged from here as a patient. Let me think, it must be nearly a year ago.' Dawes paused to consider. 'Ten months, I believe it has been, without actually checking his file. I can do that. I can pull his file if the specific date is important.'

'It isn't,' Helen said. 'Not the actual date. We just needed to know he was properly discharged.'

'He was.' Doctor Dawes looked hopefully from one of them to the other. 'Has he talked to you about his health?'

'His health?' Jake repeated. 'Not really. He has a bad foot. It looks like it needs some attention.'

Dawes frowned, and changed the subject. 'As I say, he was discharged months ago. As a mental patient.'

'Are you saying,' Jake asked, 'that there are physical issues?' But Dawes' response to that question was a stony look.

'Since his discharge, Gavin has been helping me as a sort of unpaid assistant. Not so much here, but in our workshop.'

'You have a workshop?' Helen asked. 'Where they do, well, what, exactly?'

'Indeed, we do. Sort of like what you

get when you take shop in high school. They do the same sort of things. Nothing too advanced, you understand. Just the basics. We find it is excellent therapy for many of our patients. And it turned out that Gavin Rand is surprisingly good with his hands. The perfect individual to lead a bunch of amateurs working on craft projects. Ash trays, book shelves, end tables. Nothing too difficult. Gavin was good at all that. Unlike me, I should say. Personally, I couldn't carve a straight stick out of a bar of soap.'

Now Helen laughed. 'Sounds like me, I'm afraid,' she said.

Dawes nodded knowingly. His somber expression seemed to announce that he was done with all frivolity. 'I quite understand. But Gavin was a natural. He seemed to know how things were done on an instinctive level, but even more importantly, how to teach others to do them.'

'This workshop,' Jake said. 'Do you think we could see it?'

'The actual room? I can't think why not. If you think it might help in any way,' Dawes said.

Jake shrugged. 'Probably not. But you never know. Sometimes the important answer lies in getting a picture of the person, and you never know where the telling detail is going to come from. I'd like to have a look at it anyway, if I may.'

'Of course.' Dawes got up from behind his desk. 'Come with me.'

6

Helen had learned long ago that sometimes Jake liked to just contemplate a scene in silence and see if anything jumped out at him.

So, Helen too was silent, and Dawes, perhaps because it was a part of his professional technique, was the same. The three of them stood without talking in the empty work shop, looking around.

A clock on the wall ticked noisily. Somewhere distant, a dog howled. Within, the smells were those to be expected in a work shop: sawdust, paint, machine oil. Particles of dust danced in the beams of light that spilled from a window high above in one wall, making it evident no one had been here for some time.

Dawes took a pipe from his pocket, and striking a big wooden match on the doorframe, lit it. He puffed thoughtfully on it. He looked, Helen thought, more than ever like Santa Claus.

It was Jake himself who finally broke the silence. 'Sorry,' he said. 'If there's anything to be found here, I don't see it. Or, wait, I do have one question, I guess. This place seems not to have been used for a while. Quite a while, it seems to me. Did Gavin Rand stop teaching work shop?'

'I don't think he has been here for some days,' Dawes said. 'A couple of weeks, actually. A lot of the patients were disappointed, of course. But Rand was a volunteer. I couldn't exactly force him to show up here if he did not want to.'

'But why wouldn't he want to?' Helen asked. 'What had changed?'

'I have no idea,' Dawes said, but in a voice that said he knew perfectly well why not; he just was not going to share that information with them.

'And you say this was unpaid work for Gavin?' Jake asked, deciding that on the subject of Gavin's absence they were barking up a tree that was never going to give them any harvest. 'The shop stuff?'

'Yes. Everything he did was,' Dawes said; he sounded relieved by the change of subject. 'Well, I should probably correct myself. It was unpaid as far as the payroll department is concerned. They balked at letting me have a paid helper. They said it is not in the budget. And I told Gavin that, but he did not seem to care.'

'That's what he told us, too,' Jake said.

But, Helen found herself thinking, he did care about something, enough to stop what he was doing, something he was good at and presumably liked doing. Which, for someone like Gavin Rand, would surely have taken some serious motivation. She wished Dawes were not so reticent. She felt sure the doctor could tell them all sorts of things. But he was not going to share whatever he knew with them.

'However, for the record,' Dawes went on, 'I have managed, since he started working for me, to see that his room and board are taken care of. His work was worth way more than that, of course, but at least it's something.'

'In my opinion,' Dawes said after a significant silence, 'if it were to happen,

Gavin Rand would make an excellent therapist. He is a bit fragile, emotionally, but he is certainly bright enough, and more important is that he has a natural empathy for others. Which is half the battle right there.'

'I think you're right,' Helen said, wondering all the while what it was that Dawes knew but was not telling them. Something, she felt sure; something that the Doctor very much wanted them to know, only not from him.

'Well, we don't need to take up any more of your time,' Jake said. He was frustrated by the doctor's inability to tell them anything more than the basic facts, though he had certainly been aware of this barrier before they came. Still, even if you knew the mountain was never going to move, you could always hope for a miracle, couldn't you? 'It was the discharge thing we mostly were wondering about. I guess we could have just telephoned, but I like to see people face to face when I'm asking them things. Even if the answer is going to be no answer.'

'I understand,' Dawes said, smiling a knowing smile. 'I feel the same way.'

But before Jake and Helen could leave the work shop, the doctor said, 'You know, I have been thinking: I can't, as I said, discuss the doctor-patient relationship between Gavin Rand and myself, but apart from that, he has been my assistant for the better part of a year, both in my office and here in this shop, and there is nothing unethical about my forming an opinion of him in those regards. Or in sharing that opinion with you.'

'Sounds reasonable to me,' Jake said, brightening. 'And what is that opinion?'

'My opinion is that Gavin Rand does not have it in him to hurt a fly, let alone another human being.' He hesitated for a moment. 'To be frank, and here I am going beyond what I should say, not only was he discharged as a patient long ago, but in my professional opinion he should never have been committed here in the first place. But don't tell anybody I told you that, please. I am violating my ethical rules by saying it, but the truth is, someone made a great mistake.'

'There is one more thing I just thought of,' Jake said. 'You said you had taken care of Gavin's room and board. Do you mean he's been living here at the hospital?'

'No,' Dawes said. 'I have an old friend who runs a rooming house. It's very near here, in fact. He's been staying there and I have been paying his rent. Which is minimal, in case you are puzzled. I do well here, but I don't think you could call me a wealthy man.'

'Out of curiosity, did he know you were paying the rent?' Jake asked.

Dawes shook his head. 'No, I doubt that he even suspected that's how it was. I am sure he thought the hospital was taking care of it. I never told him otherwise, certainly. He was a proud young man. And sometimes a very stubborn one. If he had thought for a moment he was living on my charity, he would probably have slept on the street instead.'

'I wonder, do you think we might see his room, where he stayed?' Jake asked.

'I don't see why not. To be honest, I think you should, it might provide you with some valuable insights. I'll give you the address. It's only a couple or three blocks from here, if you want to leave your car in the lot and walk. It'll probably save you time if you do and I'll validate your parking. In the meantime, I'll call his landlady and tell her to expect you. That would be a Mrs. Hurst.'

7

'Jake,' Helen asked when they were out on the street outside the hospital, following the directions the doctor had given them, 'why are we going to look at Gavin's rooming house? Are you expecting to find something significant there?'

'Probably not,' Jake said. 'We are trying to help this guy out of a jam, aren't we? Anything might show up. And you never know when something is going to prove useful. Didn't the good doctor hint at that?'

'Why did he suddenly lose interest in his shop classes?' Helen said. 'That seemed a bit strange to me.'

'Yes, I wondered about that too. And I think the doc knew the reason for it. But I also think he did not want to tell us what that reason was. Maybe we'll get an answer to that question where he lived. Maybe that's what he was trying to tell us, without telling us.'

As the doctor had said, it wasn't far. Much of the first block or two they traversed was taken up by professional buildings — mostly, it seemed, satellites of the hospital: medical labs, x-ray facilities, billing offices. By the third block, they found themselves in a largely residential neighborhood.

The house number they were looking for was in the fourth block. They found it with no difficulty. It turned out to be well-maintained California bungalow, recently painted an off white. As they went up the walk that led to the front door, the sounds of a party spilled out of an open window on the second floor.

'Sounds festive,' Jake said, ringing the doorbell.

'This close to the hospital, it's probably med students,' Helen said. 'They like to let their hair down. I've known a few, and they love to do it, any chance they get. By let their hair down, I mean way down. You'd be surprised if I told you some of the things I've been involved in with med students.'

'I doubt that,' Jake said, grinning.

The doorbell was answered so quickly that they could only suppose Mrs. Hurst had been waiting just inside for them to arrive. She was a little woman, no more than five one or two, and pretty; younger than they had expected and with a fragile, china doll appearance. She was drying her hands on her apron as she opened the door.

'Hi. David, Doctor Dawes, that is, phoned to say you were on your way,' she greeted them warmly. 'He thought you might be detectives, but he wasn't altogether sure.'

'We're just friends,' Jake said. 'Do you have a few minutes?'

'Of course. Come in.' She swung the door wide. 'David said you wanted to see Gavin's room. It's right along here, on this floor.' She led them past a wooden staircase going up.

'Someone's having a good time,' Jake said, glancing upward. The sounds of the party upstairs were even louder in here. Rock music and a babble of mostly male voices.

'My boys,' she said with a patient sigh.

'Med students, mostly. You know how they can be.'

Jake shot Helen a quick glance. Helen resisted the temptation to smirk. Did she know her male animals, or did she know her male animals?

Mrs. Hurst paused at a door just past the stairs and, taking a ring of keys from the pocket of her apron, fitted one of them into the lock. 'That's why I put Gavin down here,' she explained. 'He isn't like the rest of them. Not so much of a party person, if you know what I mean. Of course, he's older, too, than most of the boys upstairs, which I am sure makes a difference. Here you are.' She swung the door wide. 'But I don't know what you expect to find.'

'Probably nothing,' Jake said.

'Which is probably right,' she said. 'Gavin always kept the place neat as a pin. Again, unlike the med students.'

The room she showed them was mostly unimpressive. Except that it was neater and cleaner than some, it looked to Helen much like every room she had ever seen in a boarding house. Through an open door in one wall she could see a bit of white porcelain — the bathroom, she supposed.

Most of the space in the room they were in was taken up with an ancient wood veneer bedroom suite that looked as if it had come from some thrift shop and almost certainly did not qualify as antique: matching nightstands on either side of a bed with a metal frame twisted to more or less simulate vines and painted white; a small vanity with drawers down either side and a big round mirror above; and a chiffonier.

There was an old and surprisingly comfortable looking leather chair, near a somewhat battered roll top desk, its top rolled up just now to reveal a writing surface with a bright green blotter and not much else.

The bed was covered with a faded blue chenille spread. The wallpaper was a cascade of oversized pink roses against a gray background, and the wooden floor had several small braided and multicolored rugs scattered here and there.

A tiny kitchen nestled in one corner.

Helen went to that and opened the door to the small refrigerator. There was nothing there but three bottles of beer, different brands that no doubt had once belonged to six packs of their own kin.

'Doesn't look like he had much interest in food,' Helen said, closing the refrigerator door.

'I supplied his meals,' she said. 'That is, when he could be bothered to eat. Which was not all the time. You're right, he never seemed to have much interest in food. Or much of anything it seemed to me. He was always so impatient, as if he had to be somewhere else. Or perhaps it was things he had to do, though I don't know what they might have been, frankly.'

She looked around the room, frowning. 'That's odd,' she said, speaking more as if to herself than to them.

'What is?' Jake asked.

'A few things seem to be missing, is all I was thinking.' She looked around the room again.

'Things?' Helen asked. 'What sort of things?'

'His desk set, for one,' she said. 'It was

a very nice one. Onyx, I think. Something shiny and black, in any case. It had a pair of pens sticking out of the top. It was always there, on his desk. On the green blotter. But it's not there now.' She pointed at the small wooden desk with its exposed innards. 'And there was a picture that sat there too, next to it. Of his one-time wife, I think.'

'Dee?' Helen said and Mrs. Hurst made a grimace of distaste.

'Yes, I think that was her name,' she said, but with aversion in her voice. 'The picture was in a silver frame, which I always supposed was valuable, but that's gone, too, picture and frame both. And he had a kind of shawl, from Mexico, I think. What do they call them? I can't think of the word.'

'A serape?' Jake suggested.

'Yes, as I remember, that's what he called it. They got married there, in Mexico, he and his wife, I mean. What did you say her name was?'

'Dee,' Helen said again.

'Yes, Dee. That's right.' Her head bobbed up and down. 'He kept the shawl, the serape thing, on the chair over there, the leather one, and it's not there now.'

'You sound very familiar with the room,' Jake said. 'And its contents.'

She blushed and looked suddenly shy. 'I used to clean for him, too, once a week. And sometimes I could get him to sit quietly and drink a cup of tea with me, though as I said he always seemed as if he was about to run off someplace. So, yes, I was in here fairly often. Things get to be familiar to you, over time, you know.'

It suddenly dawned on Helen: she and Gavin were lovers. Well, it made sense, she thought: Gavin was not an unattractive young man, and she was certainly pretty enough. 'Is there a Mister Hurst, by the way?' she asked on an impulse. 'Just curious.'

'There is. What's left of him, anyway,' she said, avoiding Helen's eyes.

'What's left of him?' Helen repeated, puzzled.

'That does sound nonsensical, doesn't it?' she said with an embarrassed laugh. 'What I meant was that my husband was in an automobile accident several years

97

ago. Rather a bad one, I'm afraid. It left him in a wheelchair. He's a quadriplegic.'

'Arms and legs?' Jake asked. 'Everything gone?'

'His spinal cord was severed. Oh, they're still there, the arms and legs, they just don't function,' she said. 'Nothing much does, frankly. And, he's unable to work, of course. Or to do much of anything. That's why I let rooms. He gets disability, but it's not a lot. It's hard to get by on that.'

Much of anything, Helen repeated in her mind. Which explained a great deal, she supposed.

'These items that are missing from the room, here,' Jake said, 'he might have sold them, don't you suppose? Or pawned them.'

'I suppose he might have,' she said. 'But why would he do that? He never mentioned needing money. I'd have given him money, if he had asked. I know I sort of gave the impression that money is scarce, but we're not that hard up. Honest. And he knew that. He never did ask for money, of course. He's too proud,

I suppose. And he's always lived a kind of simple lifestyle.'

She suddenly turned on them, those blue eyes flashing with anger. 'But where is he? Why are you even here, looking at his things? You haven't told me. And I haven't seen him for two days. Has something happened to him?'

'The last we saw him, he was all right,' Jake said. 'A little tired, but . . . ' He shrugged.

'But where is he?' she demanded again. 'You haven't said where he is.'

'In Burbank,' Helen said softly.

She looked as if Helen had punched her. 'With them, you mean?' she said in a tiny voice.

'The Carters, yes,' Helen said. 'The family.'

'They're not his family.' She fairly spat the words. 'They're just a family that he married into. A long time ago.'

'You're right,' Helen said.

'He's with her, that's what you mean, isn't it?' she said. 'The ex-wife. What did you say her name was?'

'Dee.' Helen said yet again and

suppressed a smile.

'Yes, Dee. I don't know why I can't remember her name,' she said.

I'll bet I could think of reasons, Helen thought, but kept the thought to herself.

'He is with her, isn't he?' the landlady persisted. 'That's what you're really saying, when you say family?'

'He went to see her, yes,' Jake said.

'But he hasn't yet,' Helen quickly added. 'He hasn't seen her, I mean. She wasn't there when he got to the house. It's kind of complicated.'

'I hope he never does see her,' she said vehemently. 'She was so mean to him in the past.'

'I think Dee is mean to everybody,' Helen said. 'I guess you could call her an equal opportunity ogre.'

'Mrs. Hurst,' Helen started, but she interrupted her.

'Gemma,' she said. 'You can call me Gemma. That's what he called me.'

'Gemma, then, you mustn't worry yourself over Dee.'

'Mustn't I?' Her question was mocking. 'She's the one, you know, who had him committed in the first place. She told people all kinds of horrible things. But they were lies, everything she said. He wasn't like that, not at all. Gavin is such a sweet young man. So gentle, so kind. I'd hate to think of her getting her claws into him again. I think she would destroy him.'

'She might,' Helen said. 'She very well might. Dee's a destructive person.'

'Sorry to harp on them, but the things that are missing,' Jake said in a business-like voice, obviously trying to change the subject, 'Let's say that he pawned them. Is there a pawn shop nearby, do you know?'

She thought for a moment. 'There is a place on Eighth Street. It's walking distance from here. Duggan's, it's called. That's probably where he would have taken them. If he actually did pawn them.'

'Can you think of any better explanation?' Jake asked.

'No,' she said in a bitter tone of voice. 'I suppose they could have been stolen, but his room is always locked when he's not here. And besides, if he was going to see the family, he'd have wanted to have some money. He's a proud young man.

He'd never have gone there with his pockets empty.'

She sat down suddenly in the leather chair, so suddenly and so hard that the chair's frame squeaked in protest. She dropped her face into her hands and a second or two later, Helen realized she was crying, her shoulders shaking though she made not a sound.

'He was only planning a brief visit in Burbank,' Helen said. 'He'll be back here soon, I'm sure.'

'You don't understand.' She lifted a tear-stained face to look at Helen with an angry expression. 'He won't come back. Not here. Not to me. I'll never see him again.'

'He's sick, isn't he,' Jake said, suddenly realizing the truth.

'He's dying,' she said, jumping to her feet. And now the sobs came, wracking her body with their violence. She stood in the middle of the cheaply furnished room, fists clenched at her sides, and shook with the storm of her grief.

'He has cancer,' she cried in a broken voice. 'He'll be dead soon. That's why he wanted to see her, to try to straighten things out about their child. He even asked me if I would be willing to raise the boy. Of course I would. I told him that. But I begged him not to go, not to face her. He doesn't have all that long. I wanted him to stay here, where I could take care of him. He can't take care of himself. He doesn't want to admit it, but that's the truth: he can't. Not anymore. He can barely get out of the tub by himself.'

'He'll be back,' Jake said, but in a voice that said he didn't believe it either. She sat back down heavily in the leather chair and buried her face again in her hands.

'I'm sorry,' Jake said. 'I think you probably would prefer to be alone.'

'I would, yes,' she said, her voice muffled by the hands she had clapped over her face. 'If you don't mind.'

'We'll see ourselves out,' Jake said, and at the door, Helen said, 'Thank you for your time.'

'She's in love with him,' Helen said when they were outside.

Almost certainly, she was thinking, it

was Mrs. Hurst Gavin had meant when he said he had someone else in mind to raise his son. Yes, she had even said she would take Gavin's child in. And a little boy might be very good for her, therapeutic. She was going to need something to fill that empty space his leaving was going to create. Helen knew all about those empty spaces.

She thought of the two of them, Gavin and Gemma, together. They must have made love; probably many times. An image popped into her mind, of a naked Gavin sleeping in their bed; she pushed it relentlessly away, but it came back, like a ghost to haunt her.

But what dream could she have had, nurtured like a candle in the rain, so long as her husband was alive? Maybe this was why people committed murders. She could almost understand it. Except she thought the woman was in love with her husband, too. Was that possible, loving two men at the same time, maybe in different ways?

But supposing that was so, what could she have hoped for, those times when they were coupled together. Because she knew that hope was what the heart fed on. Without hope there was nothing but the darkness.

Still, telling others of the great lost love could be very appealing. She knew people who had dined out on it for years. That was a cynical way of looking at things, true, but sometimes life made you a bit cynical.

'The landlady, you mean?' Jake asked. 'In love with Gavin? Yes, it seemed that way to me too.'

'Yes, she is in love with Gavin, I'm sure of it. Only, I think she still loves her husband too. And love without sex is Jesus without the devil. They are partners, you know. If you want one, you are going to have to deal with the other.'

'I would imagine you are right. I believe she is in love with both of them. But they are two different things, you know. Love is not one thing alone. It comes in many variations. We try to define love, but how can we?'

And just like that, Helen understood anew why she was in love with this man.

'Ghosts,' Helen said. 'They're all ghosts.'

'All who?'

'Those people we have idealized. They don't exist, not in the real world. They're just phantoms in our minds. We love them because we create them.'

★ ★ ★

'Helen,' Jake said when they got back to the truck, sounding tentative, as if he was afraid he might step on toes, 'those people back in Burbank, the Carters: from what you've told me, they hurt you before, didn't they?'

Jake thought for a minute. 'I guess what I'm trying to say is, don't get too involved.'

'In what?' Helen asked.

'In any of it. That's all I am saying. I don't want you to be hurt again.'

'I'm not involved,' Helen said quickly.

Which they both knew was untrue. She was involved, had been since they had first seen that sorry figure trudging along the side of that street in Burbank. Probably long before then, even. And since then there was that broken hearted woman they had just left. And Annie.

All those knots. It was like, well, like that macramé class she had taken a while back. Only these knots were people, human beings. If one of them slipped, or she tied it wrong, it wasn't just that some flower pot would hang askew.

She could not escape the conviction that some of those strings had long since slipped through his fingers. Annie, for instance; how could she have been so wrong about her? And Gavin? It was no use excusing herself because she had been young when she and Gavin were first acquainted. She had not been so young that she did not know a troubled soul when she met one.

Or even Dee? Maybe she had gotten that knot wrong too. She had been so busy hating Dee, she had never stopped to consider that maybe Dee was hurting too, acting out her pain and grief in her own way? People did not set out at the beginning planning to be evil. They were just pursuing their happiness, like everyone else, and they went down the wrong path to get there. But maybe it was the only path they saw open to them, the only available route to get to their destination. Which was the same destination for everyone, was it not?

You had two little girls, both of them raised in the same family, the same house, even, and look how differently they had turned out. Nurture over nature, or the other way around? Or maybe neither one, really, maybe it was just some cosmic coincidence, just a random throw of the dice, something in the air that affects one person's brain and not another's, and afterward people tried to think up all kinds of excuses for it, but that was after the fact, wasn't it?

Had she even tried to understand Dee, to get to really know her? Or, and this was not the first time she'd had this thought, did nobody ever really understand anybody? Even themselves?

So maybe Dee was not evil so much as she was lost. And maybe instead of despising her she should have tried to guide her to some better place. Before it was too late. Which, surely by this time, it was.

'I'm not involved,' she said again, but this time under her breath. Because not even she believed it.

She so wanted to believe it, though.

8

They had no difficulty finding the pawn shop Gemma Hurst had told them about: Duggan's, on Eighth Street. A sign on the door said it was 'Open,' and to 'Come On In.' A bell jangled somewhere to the rear as they did so.

A man sitting on a bench at the back of the shop looked up when the bell announced their arrival. He was holding a shotgun in his hands, resting across his knees while he polished the metal to a gleam with a chamois cloth. The barrel had been sawed off short, none too expertly.

'Looks dangerous,' Jake said, nodding at the shotgun.

'It could be,' the man allowed. 'The thing is, I tried it out. Went clear down to the ocean, shot out over the water, to be safe. Found out the aim is no good. You could be shooting at your wife, and kill the cat instead.'

'That could be a blessing,' Helen said.

'Not for the cat,' the man said drily. He gave them a knowing look. 'You guys cops?'

'I used to be, but not anymore,' Jake said, 'if that's worrying you.'

'Glad to hear it. We get officers checking us out from time to time. I guess every pawn shop does. Goes with the business.'

'You're Duggan?' Jake asked.

'The man himself,' Duggan said. 'From County Cork, if you are wondering. So, then, if this is not official business, you must be shopping. Is there anything in particular I can show you?'

'A desk set, maybe,' Jake said. 'You know, the kind with a couple of pens sticking up out of it.' He had already spotted the serape, hanging over a crudely painted wooden chair. How many serapes could there be around this town?

'In onyx, maybe?' Duggan said. 'This desk set you're looking for.'

'That's the one. And while you're at it, if you've got it, a silver picture frame, with the picture of a woman in it.'

Duggan sighed wearily. 'Please tell me this stuff wasn't stolen. I'm not a fence. Not intentionally anyway. But stuff happens when you own a pawn shop. I try to screen things out, but you can't keep track of everything.'

'No, not stolen,' Jake said. 'I think the guy who brought them in was almost certainly the legitimate owner. He just wanted to raise some cash.'

Duggan nodded. 'That's usually the case, isn't it?'

'Do you remember him?' Jake asked. 'The guy who pawned those things?'

'We get a lot of people in and out, but, yeah, I think I do. A young guy, was he, nice looking, kind of a military sort, I thought. Had a bit of a limp, as I recall.'

'That sounds like him,' Helen said.

'He said his name was David Dawes,' Duggan said.

Jake scoffed derisively. 'He was pulling your leg on that part of it.'

'I didn't ask the fellow for any ID,' Duggan said. 'Sometimes I do. Sounds like I maybe should have this time.'

'David Dawes is his doctor,' Jake said.

'Or was. But I doubt it makes much difference. The stuff wasn't stolen, that's the important thing. It was all his own.'

'That's good to know,' Duggan said. 'I don't need any trouble with the law. I run a clean business.'

'Sounds like it. How about if I buy the stuff back? The desk set, the picture frame, that serape over there,' Jake said.

'Sure. Tell you what, I'll waive my usual markup, let you have it for what I gave him. Which was not a lot, by the way. None of it was worth much. I probably wouldn't have taken it at all, but he acted like he needed the dough.'

'In his mind, I think that's how he saw it,' Helen said.

'It's different if you know they're just thinking about the next bottle of Thunderbird, or something to shoot up,' Duggan said. 'I usually just send that sort on their way. But this one seemed like a nice young man. Just short on cash.'

'I don't think getting high or drunk was on Gavin's agenda,' Helen said. 'But thank you for caring.'

Jake paid the price the man gave him,

and collected the three items. The silver picture frame was empty now.

'Was there a picture in this frame when he brought it in?' Helen asked. 'Just asking.'

'There was,' Duggan admitted. 'A young woman, not bad looking, as I recall. I asked him if he wanted to keep that, but he said no, he did not want it.'

'What happened to it?' Helen asked. 'If you remember.'

'I burned it. Sorry, I hope it's not important.' Duggan looked appropriately repentant.

When they left, the bell again jangling, the proprietor was once more in his chair in the rear of the shop, back to polishing the shotgun across his knees.

★ ★ ★

'So, Cousin Dee lied, about everything,' Jake said, echoing what Helen had been thinking. They were on the freeway again, headed back to Burbank.

'It seems so. If I understood what Dawes was telling us. The important thing is, though, Gavin wasn't crazy. Not even at the beginning.'

'How did that kid come to get sent to a mental hospital anyway? If there was never anything wrong with him?'

'Exactly what you said: Dee lied. She told everyone he had attacked her. They were still married then, and they were quarreling. She was pregnant at the time. That's all true, of course. And when you base a lie on a lot of true things, verifiable things, the false part becomes believable too. But Gavin insisted he had not attacked her. He said she had scratched her own arms and given herself bruises.'

'And I suppose nobody believed him.'

'Nobody did. Would you?' Helen asked. 'Of course, in all fairness, what he said seemed at the time so unlikely. What kind of a woman would do that to herself and then blame her husband for it? No one gave his story any credence. Now, I'm not so sure. If anyone could make up something like that, it would have to be Dee.'

They drove some miles in silence, each of them lost in their own thoughts.

Helen was thinking, there was always that moment in childhood, wasn't there, when you looked out the window and saw the future out there, waving at you through the glass. Even if sometimes you didn't recognize it.

Helen glanced at her watch. 'But philosophizing takes a back seat to food, wouldn't you say? And as I remember, the Carters don't hold up dinner for anyone, for any reason. That's at six o'clock sharp. It's almost six now. Which means we're probably not going to eat with them.'

'Hey, this is Los Angeles. There's no shortage of restaurants around, seems to me. We could eat on the way. There's always some place close by.'

'You're right,' Helen agreed. 'And you know what? I do know a place, and it is close by. We're practically going past it, as a matter of fact. A nice little Italian joint: checkered tablecloths, candles in Chianti bottles. Mama is in the kitchen and her sons work the dining room. Very old fashioned. What do you think?'

'Sounds like my kind of place.'

9

Within an hour, replete, they were back on the freeway. The summer afternoon was fading. It was sunset, the sky a beautiful streaking of pink and orange, with clouds of a dark blue, almost purple.

'Los Angeles sunsets. You tend to forget it's the smog that makes the sunsets so spectacular here,' Jake said.

'It's sort of like behind every pretty picture there is an ugly reality,' Helen said.

'Sounds right to me. Oh, hey, we've got to stop here,' Jake suddenly announced. He made a quick turn, crossing over three lanes and evoking lots of honking horns. He pulled into the parking lot of a strip mall.

There was only one store in the mini mall that seemed to be open for business, though the lot was fairly full and they had to park some distance away from its door. Helen looked at the store's front windows, covered with large black lettering painted on the glass and smaller papers, sale announcements, glued on.

'Ron and Ray, Camping Supplies,' she read aloud. 'Why are we stopping here? We don't need camping supplies. Do we?'

'We need sleeping bags,' Jake said. 'We've got a guy sleeping in our bed. Remember?'

'Oh, yeah. Gavin. You're right,' she said aloud. 'We will need sleeping bags. I'll get them.'

'Get two of them,' Jake said.

'I will. But I know how we can make one big one out of the two,' Helen said. "Thanks to my training in the Girl Scouts. We used to do it all the time.

Helen sat for a moment, looking through the windshield at the far hills, purple and blue at this distance.

As if she had spoken aloud, Jake followed her gaze, looked at the distant blue ridge as well. 'I'm guessing those are the Hollywood Hills, right?'

'The Santa Monicas,' Helen said. 'The Santa Monica Mountains, officially, on the maps, if you look, but they're like the Verdugos, They're not real mountains, I mean. Not like the Rockies or the Sierras.'

Jake cracked his knuckles. 'You know, if I was a betting man, I'd bet it's going to rain. I feel it in my joints.'

'It never rains here in the summer,' Helen said, and added, thoughtfully, 'Except when it does. Which is in June, when it happens.'

'It's June now,' Jake said. 'I thought it was June gloom here, all summer long.'

'It is, mostly. But every once in a while, the clouds let loose. And when they do, it's like they've been saving it up for a while, it all comes down at once.'

He was watching a cloud, a ball of fluff, trying to slip across the distant Santa Monica Mountains. But one high peak caught it, tore and bruised its underside, leaving blue black shreds trailing after. There was a sudden clatter of fronds from the palm trees along the street, and the wind hummed a song it sometimes sang more lustily among the thatched peaks.

'You may be right,' Helen said. 'I think it's going to rain.'

'You might get caught.'

'If it starts while I'm inside, I'll just wait it out. These summer storms never last long. It comes down so hard that water is all used up in no time.'

The rain, which almost never fell in Los Angeles in the summertime, began just as Helen got out of the truck, a few scattered drops to start, but before Helen had even reached the entrance to the camping supply store it had become a downpour.

She ran the last couple of feet and burst into the store through its glass doors. She got the sleeping bags and paid for them, and walked back to the front door with one under each arm. Outside, the rain was still coming down in sheets.

★   ★   ★

By the time Jake and Helen had driven back to Burbank, it looked as if it would never rain again. As it seldom did, in Los Angeles, in the summer.

10

Annie had always been a nurturer; a frustrated nurturer, to be sure, having never found anyone who wanted to be nurtured. But the instinct had never left her. She had tried, when they had been small children, to nurture her sister Dee, who, though two years older than her, had always possessed an infantile quality that made her seem forever a baby. And Dee could be seen at anybody's knowing glance to want taking care of.

As it turned out, however, Dee did not want to be taken care of by her younger sister. To Dee's mind, Annie was a competitor. A daughter also of the same parents, she might reasonably expect them to love her as much and in the same way as they did Dee.

Dee, however, from her earliest years, was disinclined to share anyone's love, or even their affection. She had made it her goal, her Unholy Grail it might almost be called, to ensure not only that her parents loved her, but that they loved her alone. So far as familial affection was concerned, Annie could fend for herself, the way Dee saw things.

When their mother, Paula, was alive, Dee was only partially successful. She was successful with her father, certainly. By the time Dee was seven, and Annie five, Dee had convinced her father that the sun rose and set for her and her alone. Doug scarcely remembered, then or after, that he even had a second daughter.

A mother is a different sort of creature, however. Paula loved her second daughter, if not with quite the same delight, then certainly no less resolutely than she loved the first. For all her love, however, Paula was a woman of poor health, and by the time she might have made a real difference in Annie's life, she was gone.

Probably only Annie alone truly mourned her. For the others, Paula had been little more than a convenience, a means to whatever end. For Dee, simply another means of getting her way.

For Annie, however, she had been a

source of love, a love that for the most part dried up and blew away when her mother was gone, leaving her with empty rooms in an empty house.

Until, at least, Helen had shown up. Though she would have died before admitting it, young Annie had developed the most serious crush on her older cousin. A cousin who seemed, like everyone else in the family: unaware of her very existence. Or, if not of her existence, certainly of her affection.

In time, of course, there was the widow, Mrs. Ricketts, hired by Doug to fill some of the empty space left by Paula's going. Mrs. Ricketts had scarcely set foot in the house before Dee, who decided that the new woman in their midst would end up as either her ally or a foe, had set herself to seducing her as well. So successful was her campaign that in no time at all, Mrs. Ricketts had come to think of Dee as her 'little girl,' and Annie as nothing more than an interloper. Annie might almost not have been a member of the same family.

But Douglas Carter was a virile man, if

often a silly one. Like many survivors, he secretly blamed the deceased for her death. And he sorely missed not his wife's company nor her keen intelligence nor even the love that she bestowed without stint on all of her family. What he missed, and that most sorely, was the convenience of having a bed partner.

And that need the stolid Mrs. Ricketts was not likely to fulfill even had she been willing. Like Dorothy Parker's porcupine, she defended what no one was after.

So Douglas married a second time, this time to a much younger woman, the very pretty and herself rather childlike Lois Tyler. Lois, though no match for her predecessor in intelligence, was no fool, either. She was marrying into a family that, if not exactly wealthy by Beverly Hills standards, was hardly in straits, either. Mostly on its own, Doug's construction business did well, and Paula herself had come from a family of some means, and so she had brought a not inconsiderable bit of money to their marriage.

Not only was this family well off, then,

but it was a family as well in which, Lois quickly perceived, there were two sources of power. One of them was the old lady, Doug's mother: Grannie, to the two small girls, and Aunt Grace to Helen Feather when she came to stay for a brief time.

The other power was a joint one between Dee, the oldest child, and the housekeeper, Ricketts, who had by this time established herself as the true mistress of the household, though she was careful in all matters to seem to defer to the family matriarch, the girls' Grannie. The task of deferment got easier as the years passed, and the older woman became less authoritative and more reticent herself.

Annie might have set herself to nurturing her grandmother, but Mrs. Ricketts and Dee were two steps ahead of her in this, as in most possibilities. To have allowed a partnership to form between those two might have been to have their own authority in the household challenged, and both were too wily to have allowed this to happen. So it did not. By the time she was eight years old, Annie had become, for all intents and purposes, an outsider in her own family, and so she remained.

As a result of all this, and except for one or two individuals she met while at school and who sometimes described her as 'Mother Ducky,' Annie's nurturing nature had remained largely unfulfilled. There was simply no one in her family who needed, or even much wanted, her love. And she had long been molded to believe certain things about herself, some of them unfortunate.

She believed, for example, what she had always been told, especially by her beautiful sister, that she was the ugly duckling of the family, certainly when compared to that same sister. Her father thought so. Her stepmother seemed to agree. And even the housekeeper was of that opinion, and not above saying so, though carefully when no one was at hand to hear her pronouncements.

Alone now in the house after Jake and Helen had gone, Annie went to the bedroom in the rear. Gavin Rand was sound asleep by this time. Sleeping, he had a look of utter innocence about him, like that of a child. She stood for a moment, staring down at him, and something sharp and sweetly painful seemed to pierce her heart.

She had always taken for granted, without consciously dwelling upon it, that somehow, without even knowing how it had come about, she had become her older sister's stooge. Now, looking down at the sleeping man, she realized that he shared her lot. He was as much Dee's victim as she had been; perhaps even more so.

She suddenly knew, with such certainty that she could not for a moment ever again doubt it, that Dee had lied about seeing her ex-husband running away on that awful night. Perhaps she had even lied about what supposedly had happened earlier between them: that alleged assault which had resulted in his being sent to a mental hospital.

Gavin Rand had always insisted that he had done nothing, that Dee had inflicted the wounds upon herself. Of course, no one had believed him. His claim seemed so unlikely.

Only, it was not really unlikely, not to anyone who saw Dee honestly, for what she was. It was exactly the kind of thing she would do, Annie found herself thinking.

But, if that were true, and she little doubted now that it was, then this poor young man had been twice Dee's hapless victim; and this time, he might well pay for her crimes with his life.

She suddenly realized that, whatever Helen and her friend might try to do, there was only one person who could prevent that from happening: and that was she. She made herself a solemn vow that she would do so, somehow. Though at the moment she had no idea whatsoever of how she might accomplish that goal.

She left the young man asleep and returned to the downstairs room, to await her family's arrival.

11

Jake and Helen had not long since driven out of the driveway on their way to that hospital in Santa Monica than Doug Carter arrived home in a sort of convoy of three cars. Not only did the entire family and their housekeeper come into the house in his wake, but close on their heels came the local Chief of Police, Dan Tyler, with four dark suited men following him.

'Aha,' Doug said to the room in general, holding a duffel bag aloft, 'Look, everybody, what we found in the bushes down by the gate. Show them, Chief. This proves the madman was here.'

The police chief took the duffel bag from him. 'It's his, all right,' he said, holding it up in turn for everyone to see. 'No question about it. It's even got his identification inside. So I guess Mister Carter is correct, this does prove he was here.'

'And me too,' Dee said brightly. 'I'm the one who saw him.'

'Yes, darling, you were right,' Doug said. 'No one ever doubted you.'

Annie suppressed an urge to groan aloud. Now how on earth had that happened, the duffel bag left in the bushes? She would have to ask Helen for some kind of explanation. Gavin had arrived here earlier with them. Surely they must know why his duffel bag was in the shrubs down by the gate. It seemed such an odd thing, and indeed incriminating. Maybe Dee was telling the truth after all. But that was even more unlikely, it seemed to her.

'Burke,' Chief Tyler addressed the suited man closest to him, 'Go around the house and close all the shutters.'

'Goodness gracious. We'll be baked alive,' Grannie muttered, but no one paid her any mind. 'With everything sealed up. Am I the only one with sense enough to know it's hot outside? Ricketts, I think I would like a glass of iced tea, if you would be so kind.'

'Yes, ma'am, I'll bring it right in,'

Ricketts said. 'Anyone else? Dee, my love, would you like one? Or you, Miss Annie?'

Dee gave a toss of her head which Ricketts seemed to understand was a no. Annie took a moment to think. 'No, nothing for me,' she decided.

'Very good. I'll be right back, Mrs. Carter,' Ricketts said. She disappeared into the kitchen.

With a nod but no words, Burke set about doing as he had been instructed, starting with the big front room, where he firmly closed and latched all the shutters over the windows, leaving the room in semi-gloom.

Annie had been sitting demurely on the sofa when they came in ('You stay here,' Helen had instructed her. 'It's your job to see that no one disturbs our sleeping intruder.') When she saw Burke start toward the kitchen, she called after him, 'There are no shutters in that back bedroom. Save yourself the bother of checking.'

'Right, thanks,' he called in return.

Nevertheless, on an impulse, Annie followed Burke into the kitchen, and stood watching from the doorway while he closed the shutters over the two windows there. She had a moment's fright when he went onto the landing to the cellar stairs, but she managed to keep her voice calm and said, 'No shutters on the cellar windows, either.'

'Oh, right,' he said, and came back into the kitchen.

'How am I supposed to see to cook?' Ricketts asked from the sink where she was filling a glass with tap water. She had already added a powdered mix to the glass. If Dee had wanted some, she would have taken the time to brew fresh tea and chill it with cubes, but the instant mix and tap water was good enough for the old lady, in her opinion. She stirred the brew in the glass and glowered at the shuttered windows.

Wordlessly, Burke flicked on the overhead light as he left the room. Annie trailing behind him, smiled to herself when he did so. She had never liked Ricketts.

'Okay,' the Chief said when Burke had returned, 'I want you men to take all four corners of the house outside, and needless to say, no one gets inside.'

'I'm not afraid if he does,' Doug said. He took a handgun out of his jacket pocket. 'Let him try anything, is what I say.'

'Oh, Doug, dear,' Grannie said, taking the glass of tea Ricketts brought her, 'I don't think that's such a good idea. The last time you fired that thing we lost a window.' She took a sip of the tea and made a face, and set it aside, but said nothing.

'Your mother is right, Mr. Carter,' the Chief said. 'My men here are all armed. Leave the firearms up to the professionals.'

Grumbling under his breath, Doug took the gun over to the credenza and dropped it into the top drawer there. 'I'd hate to think that madman might get inside, and we'd be here with no protection,' he said. 'Simply at his mercy. A lunatic, as we all know.'

'He won't get in,' Tyler insisted. 'My men will see to that.'

'Huh,' Doug merely grunted. Annie

breathed a sigh of relief to see the drawer closed with the gun in it.

'Chief,' Annie said, walking up to him and lowering her voice, 'I wonder if I could have a word with you, in private?' She thought if she could talk to him alone, explain about Gavin's presence, he might be receptive to seeing Gavin did not get shot.

'Later, maybe,' he said. 'Right now I've got to think of that madman on the loose, the one who left my sister in a coma.'

Annie groaned inwardly. She had forgotten that her stepmother, Lois, was the chiefs sister.

'But you don't actually know it was him,' she said on a hopeful note.

Doug, standing nearby, heard her. 'Dee saw him,' he said. 'Running away. Why would he be running away if he hadn't done anything?'

'If he *was* running away,' Annie said, but no one seemed even to hear her. She could not very well tell them he probably did not have the strength to run. That would require explanations that she was not yet prepared to give. 'You know, Dad, maybe you're just biased.'

'Now you just listen to me, little girl,' Doug said angrily, 'No one can say I am prejudiced. You were too young to remember, I suppose, when that first colored family moved into a house not two blocks from here. There was a lot of flak among the neighbors, let me tell you. And I was the one who said, 'Let them be. They have as much right to be here as we do, regardless of whether or not they are our class of people.' So kindly don't go calling me prejudiced.'

'I stand corrected,' Annie said.

'I'll tell you one thing,' Chief Tyler said, 'Doug, here, Mr. Carter, has got the right idea. If I see this loony, I'll do what he says, I'll shoot first and ask questions later.'

'My sentiments exactly,' Doug said, pulling the credenza drawer open again.

'Close that drawer, back up, Mr. Carter,' Tyler ordered.

Doug swore under his breath, but he closed the drawer obediently.

12

It was growing dark by the time Jake and Helen arrived back at the house in Burbank, driving up the curving drive to the gravel lot in front.

'I wonder . . . ' Jake said as they climbed out of the truck.

'Wonder what?' Helen asked, walking carefully on the well combed gravel, as if not to disturb the stones.

'I'm thinking, if we could get Gavin out of the house, we could stash him someplace safer.'

'Maybe even back at his boarding house,' Helen said with enthusiasm. 'I'm sure we would make Gemma happy if we showed up with Gavin in tow.' Then her face fell. 'But how could we do that? Looks like the family is in there. We can't very well just walk him right past them and out the front door.'

'I'm thinking we take him out a window,' Jake said.

'There's men standing there at the front of the house, at both the corners,' Helen said, nodding in their directions. 'At a guess, I'd say they're keeping an eye on the place. On who comes and goes.'

'Probably. But it looks to me like they're watching the front. Gavin is in our room and that's in the back, isn't it? Neither of these guys could see the window in our room. If we took Gavin out that window . . . '

'And did what with him? If we brought him around here, to the truck, they'd be sure to see us then. To see him.'

'There must be another house back there. Maybe we could take him across their yard.'

'There's a fence. I remember that.'

'What kind of fence? Metal? Barbed wire? Electrified?'

'As I recall, it used to be an old fashioned wooden one,' Helen said. 'A picket fence.'

'Which we could get across easily enough. Hell, I could probably lift the guy over it, if I had to.'

'There would still be the problem of

getting him to the truck, only instead of getting across one yard, we'd have two to contend with.'

'If there's a house back there, there must be a street too. Suppose you stayed there with him, in the neighbor's yard, and I brought the truck around to the next street. We could have him out of the place and no one would ever have to know he had even been here.'

'True, but, uh, just as a matter of curiosity, Jake, what if Gavin didn't want to go?'

'In that case, we hog-tie him and carry him out. Look, it's for his own good.'

'People always say that.'

'Helen, he's not safe there. You know that as well as I do, maybe better. Annie says her dad is going to shoot him on sight.'

Helen thought for a minute. 'It's worth checking, I suppose,' she said. 'At least we can see if the coast is clear. Wait, where are you going?'

'No time like the present, I always say.' Jake was already on his way around the house. There was a man in a charcoal colored suit standing at the corner. The bulge in his jacket told Jake he was probably armed.

'Evening,' Jake said as they went past him, and Helen waved with her fingers and said, 'Hi. Nice night.'

The suited man did not reply, nor did he make any move to stop them, but his eyes followed them around the corner.

'He was watching us very carefully,' Helen whispered when they were well past.

'But from where he's standing, he wouldn't be able to see us in the rear, would he?'

'If there's guards posted in the front, wouldn't they have posted some in the back too?'

'Only one way to find out.'

They came to a back corner of the house. It was dark here. In the front, there was a porch light over the door to provide a faint glow of illumination but there was no light in the rear.

'See anyone?' Jake asked, pausing.

Helen looked around. Above, the sky was dazzling with stars, but their twinkling light did nothing for the ocean of darkness that was the back yard and the moon had not yet come out to offer its assistance.

'No, not really,' Helen said. 'But there are all those trees and bushes in the rear of the lot there, and the Japanese maple outside our window. Anyone could be hiding by them.'

Jake looked, squinting. 'I don't see anyone. That's our window, halfway down, isn't it? The one with no shutters.'

Helen stood on tiptoe and looked past his shoulder. 'That's the one,' she said. 'I think. It's hard to say in the dark. But there's not much else back here. A cellar window or two, but they're down at ground level.'

'Well, let's take a closer look. I'd like to know if it's unlocked.'

They rounded the corner of the house and crept toward the window halfway along, Jake in a determined lead, Helen following less enthusiastically.

They had just gotten to the window, and Jake was trying to raise the sash, when a gun went off and something struck the side of the building far above their heads. A voice behind them said, 'The next one will be aimed lower. Hold it right there, you two.'

'Just checking to see if the window is locked,' Jake said.

'Both of you, put your backs to the wall, your hands in the air, or I'll shoot,' the voice said.

'I guess that answers that question,' Helen said. 'The one about, are there any guards back here? You know, the point I brought up.'

She turned obediently to put her back to the building's wall and her hands in the air. Beside her, Jake did the same. A dark-suited man, who might almost have been the twin of the one at the front corner of the house, came out of the darkness. He had a gun in one hand, and a flashlight in the other. He flicked the light on and flashed it in their faces.

'Look, fella,' Jake said, blinking, 'We're guests of the Carters. And could you take that light out of our eyes?'

'I'm family, as a matter of fact,' Helen said.

'Sure you are.' The stranger moved the light a few inches to the side and looked closely at both of them, and closer still at Helen. 'You don't have a lot of family resemblance, if you ask me.'

'We didn't ask,' Helen said. 'And if you don't believe me, the simplest way to settle the matter is to ask the people inside.'

The man took a moment to think that suggestion over. 'Okay, then, that's what we'll do.' He waved the gun at them. 'Come on, you two first. And no funny business.'

'I wasn't planning on my ballet routine,' Helen said, and Jake laughed aloud; but they went obediently before the man in the dark suit, back the way they had come, to the front of the house, where the guard there was standing with hands on hips, watching them approach.

'They don't look like the guy who was described to us,' he told his fellow policeman. He waved his gun at Jake and Helen again. 'Go on, you two, front door. Inside.'

Where, of course, the family, gathered

in the big room in front, was surprised to see them marching ahead of a gun.

'They were fooling around with the window in back. Looked like they were trying to break in,' the dark-suited man said.

'Well, I am sorry to spoil your fun,' Doug said, 'but the girl is family. Hello there, Helen. I don't know the big guy though.'

'This is my friend, Jake,' Helen said, glad to put her hands down without danger of being shot. She smiled over her shoulder at the man with the gun. 'Satisfied?' she asked.

'Just doing my job,' the man said, holstering his gun.

'At least we know your men are on their toes,' Grannie said to Chief Tyler. 'If these two couldn't get in, most likely the crazy one can't either.'

Doug frowned at Helen. 'But what were you doing messing around with that window anyway?'

'We just wanted to be sure it was locked,' Jake said.

'But wouldn't that have been easier to

do from inside?' Doug asked.

'It would. Of course it would,' Jake agreed. 'Only . . . ' He paused, stymied.

'Only, we were outside,' Helen said quickly, 'When we thought about checking it. And you know what they say: there's no time like the present.'

Helen had noticed that when she introduced Jake, Dee threw an appreciative glance his way.

Dream on, Helen thought wryly, and gave her an evil eye warning, which she affected not to see.

For Jake, it was his first opportunity to see and to assess the family, except for Annie, whom he quite liked. But from Annie's remarks, and Helen's, he felt as if he mostly already knew them. He would have pegged Dee right off as a spoiled brat, pretty but not exceptionally so, in his opinion; and her father as a silly man who had no judgment at all, about anything.

And then there was the grandmother, or Grannie to the girls. Her round face had probably once been pretty, too, but now it was sunken in and so lined that it reminded him of nothing so much as an old map of Los Angeles.

He was honest enough with himself to know that he felt a lot of jealousy toward these people. Or, not so much jealousy as resentment. They had been unkind to Helen, and that made him sore. So, maybe a lot of what he felt was resentment; perhaps ninety percent. Even so, that still left ten percent, and that ten percent did not like them — Annie excepted, of course. For whatever reason, she reminded him of Helen.

'I'm afraid we've already had dinner,' the old lady was saying, bringing Jake's thoughts back to the present moment, 'But I can have Ricketts fix you two a tray, if you'd like.'

'Sure,' Helen said, wanting to be congenial. It seemed as if they had already gotten off on the wrong foot. 'We can always manage a bite.'

'I know I can,' Jake said enthusiastically. And, Helen thought, he was probably serious. She had never known anyone with Jake's appetite — for everything.

'Annie, call Ricketts,' Aunt Grace said, 'And ask her to put something together.'

'Never mind,' Annie said, 'I'll take care of it.' She disappeared into the kitchen, with a smile that made Helen think she had probably guessed they had already eaten.

If she had, she had apparently also made up her mind that she was not going to let the cat out of the bag. She was back in what Helen thought an astonishingly short time, carrying a tray. She set it on a coffee table and waved her hand over it.

'Help yourselves,' she told them.

There were two small china plates on the tray that held what looked like tiny mesas of pâté with a mushroom slice on their flat tops and a yellowish aspic over them; little tarts of puff pastry fairly bursting with what appeared to be a spinach purée, and two lidded bowls which, when Annie whisked away the lids, held a pale green liquid garnished with little sprigs of dill and a dollop each of crème fraiche: 'Chilled cucumber soup,' she explained. 'Great for hot weather.'

With all this came two frosted glasses

of a chilled white wine. 'Pinot Grigio,' she informed them, handing each of them a glass.

'How on earth did you do all this so quickly?' Helen asked, taking a spoon to the cold soup. It was delicious. She forgot altogether that a moment before she had been stuffed.

'I've been taking a cooking class,' she said. 'In college.'

'I'd say you are passing it with flying colors,' Jake said, finishing off one of the little tarts in two bites.

Annie beamed happily. 'And I've been practicing since I got home.'

Ricketts, who had followed her in from the kitchen, cleared her throat noisily.

'And Rickets made the spinach tarts,' Annie added hastily. Ricketts passed a simpering smile around the room before she went back through the swinging door. Jake resisted an urge to spit his tart back out.

'Are those sleeping bags?' Doug said, looking at the bundles Jake and Helen had put aside when they sat down to eat.

'They are. Just in case,' Helen said.

'In case?' Doug raised an eyebrow. Unfortunately, Helen could think of no good explanation for the sleeping bags. No satisfactory 'in case'.

'Jake has a bad back,' Annie said.

'That's right.' Jake agreed quickly. 'Sometimes I do a lot better sleeping on the floor. These are just in case.'

'And of course, if he sleeps on the floor, so do I,' Helen said, smiling all around. She gave Dee the benefit of an especially bright grin.

Which Dee pretended not to see. She put a hand up to her face. 'Oh, I forgot,' she said, and turning toward the kitchen, she shouted, 'Ricky. Ricky, I need you.'

In a minute, Ricketts was back from the kitchen, hurrying in with her clumsy shuffling gait. 'Yes, lamb, what is it, my love?'

'I'm going to a party tonight,' Dee said. 'And I want to wear my pink dress, you know the one I mean.'

'I do indeed, and I just know you'll be the prettiest one there in that dress.'

'But it needs ironing. And I can't find the pink shoes that go with it.'

'You leave that to me, lamb. I'll see to the dress, and I will find the shoes for you. You just leave everything to your Ricky.'

Although he had heard much about her, and except for her brief appearance a few minutes earlier, this was the first time Jake had really gotten a look at Ricketts, and he gave her a good once over. Like Annie, Dee's sister, Ricketts was well padded, but while Annie was a small person, almost elfin in appearance, Ricketts was a big woman. She stood not much less than six feet tall, and was stockily built, with muddy-colored hair pulled into a tight bun on the back of her head.

When she walked, she had a way of thrusting one hip forward at a time, like a cowboy in an old oater, heading down a dirt street on his way to the gunfight. Her eyes were small, constantly in movement, so she missed very little and her mouth was set in a thin line of seeming disapproval. Only her 'little girl' elicited smiles from the housekeeper, though those were generous indeed.

'Ricketts,' Annie said, catching her on

the way to the stairs, 'Last night when my stepmother was ... ' She paused, reluctant to put into words what had allegedly happened.

Ricketts, however, felt no such reluctance. 'Last night when that madman attacked her, you mean,' she said, clicking her tongue in disapproval. 'An ugly business. What about it?'

'Only, you don't actually know that's what happened, do you?' Annie said. 'I mean, you were in the kitchen, weren't you?'

'Well, I was, of course, but I heard her yell, and Miss Dee saw him running away right after, so I think it's obvious what happened,' Ricketts said.

She is Dee's slave, Helen was thinking, just as Annie had said. Whatever lie Dee told, Ricketts would support her in it.

'It's clear enough to me,' Doug said.

Annie sighed. 'I don't see how everyone is so sure, if nobody saw anything happen. And nobody did. Dee, you didn't see anything either, did you?'

'I saw Gavin,' Dee said from halfway up the stairs. 'He was running. That's all I needed to see. And Lois is in a coma, thanks to the beating he gave her. Honestly, I don't get your point, Annie. The way you talk, anyone would think you were trying to defend this crazy person.'

'Maybe he's not crazy,' Helen said.

'He was in a mental hospital,' Doug said. 'Why would he be in a mental hospital if he wasn't crazy?'

'But he was discharged, according to his doctor,' Helen said. 'Months ago.'

'Doctors can make mistakes, same as everyone else,' Doug said. 'It sounds to me like this doctor did. Or, maybe . . . ' He rubbed his thumb and fingers together, a universal symbol for bribery.

'I don't think a doctor would be likely to resort to that,' Helen said.

'It happens. In every profession,' Doug insisted. 'Even the construction trade, to be honest. I don't take them, but that's not to say they haven't been offered.'

I'll bet, Jake thought. 'And how was he going to pay a bribe, anyway?' Jake asked aloud. 'He didn't have any money of his own, did he?'

151

Doug shrugged. 'I'm just saying . . . one hears things. Nothing surprises me anymore, is all I'm saying.'

'Besides, the doctor said — ' Helen started to say, and stopped when she saw Jake give a slight shake of his head.

Jake was right, of course, they weren't supposed to tell anyone else that the doctor had said Gavin should not have been there in the first place. That could get the doctor into a lot of trouble. It was unethical, perhaps even illegal, for a doctor to share such confidences.

'The doctor said what?' Dee asked in a haughty tone of voice. She might almost have known what Helen was thinking.

'He said Gavin wouldn't hurt a fly,' Jake said quickly.

Dee gave a toss of her head. 'Which tells you how much he knows. I for one don't think that doctor's opinion is worth a hill of beans. If you want *my* opinion.'

'Doesn't sound like it to me, either,' Doug said. 'And this doctor is the one who discharged him? Goes to show you.' He once again did the business of rubbing thumb and fingers together.

'Come on, Ricky, let's go find those shoes.' Dee darted like a too self-conscious butterfly the rest of the way up the stairs, Ricketts plodding heavily after her.

'Never you worry, now, my lamb,' Ricketts said, 'You leave things to your Ricky. She'll take care of everything.' And in case anyone had missed it, she said again, emphatically, 'Everything.'

Doug went to the drawer where he had left his gun and took it out. 'I still say, this is the answer to our prowler.'

'Only if you are an expert at using that thing,' Helen said. She looked around the room at the people gathered there. Everyone looked so — she had to search for the word, so *alive*. And yet death was like a jack in the box, it could pop up at any moment with its evil grin. Who knew when the boat was waiting at the landing to carry you across the River Styx? She looked across the room at Jake, and found Jake looking hard at him.

Had he been wondering about the same boat?

'I think I'll get our room ready for

153

sleeping,' Helen said.

'I'll help,' Annie volunteered. She went with them, through the kitchen, unpeopled at the moment.

'Do you think . . . ?' she started to ask them.

'Not here,' Jake said. 'Too close to the family. Someone might hear.'

They continued on into the back bedroom, where Gavin was still asleep on the bed. Annie gave him a disapproving look.

'Still here,' Jake said. 'And in case you were wondering, the reason we were checking the window is because we were thinking of how we might get him out of the house.'

'I figured as much,' Annie said. 'No luck.'

'Not with Pistol-Packing-Papa on the prowl,' Helen said.

'So now what?'

'I'm thinking,' Jake said. 'If Gavin didn't attack Lois . . . '

'He says he didn't,' Helen pointed out.

'Right. But if he didn't, who did? For sure she didn't beat herself into a coma.'

'I know who I would like it to be,' Annie said drily.

'Dee?' Helen suggested.

'It's the sort of thing she would do,' Annie said.

'Agreed.'

'But we don't have any evidence that indicates it was Dee,' Jake said. 'The fact that the two of you don't like her is not proof of anything.'

'Well, then, who else?' Helen asked.

'Or, maybe better yet, why?' Jake said. 'If we can come up with a motive, it might point us in the right direction.' He looked at Annie. 'Any thoughts about why someone would try to crack Lois's skull?'

'No,' she said, and then, 'Well, maybe. But you didn't hear this from me.' She glowered at both of them.

'I'm very hard of hearing,' Helen said.

Annie looked at Jake. 'I'm practically stone deaf,' he said. 'What are we not hearing?'

'I heard . . . well, there was a guy I knew back in college, said he knew Lois from way back. When he was a kid, actually. He had paper route, when he was like, maybe fifteen. He said she came on to him.'

'When he was fifteen?' Helen said,

looking shocked.

'All I'm saying,' Annie said, 'is that he said she tried to seduce him. He says he turned her down, but I always had the impression he was a habitual liar, so that may not be altogether accurate.'

'Hmm.' Jake thought for a moment. 'So, not a woman much concerned with morals, sounds like to me.' He looked long and hard at Annie. 'What is your impression of her? More recently, I mean.'

'You mean, since she married my father?'

'Exactly. Do you think she was faithful to her vows?'

Annie kind of fidgeted. 'I don't really know . . . '

'But you suspect something?'

'There were times when my father wasn't here, and I would see Lois, and she had this, you know, this kind of glow that some women get after, you know . . . '

She glanced at Jake and then lowered her eyes. 'It was just an impression that I had, though. I can't say anything for certain.'

'Of course not,' Jake agreed. 'But, just out of curiosity, do you have any thoughts about who might have been responsible for that glow?'

She looked up at the ceiling with a contemplative expression, as if she expected to see an answer written up there.

'Well,' she said, after a long, thoughtful pause. 'Danton Rhodes seemed to be around a lot at the time.'

'Danton Rhodes?' Helen echoed the name. 'Who is he?'

'As I understand it,' she said, 'he's the man Dee is going to marry. See, she has to be married on her twenty-first birthday to inherit the trust Mother left for her.' She gave Helen a frank look. 'But, I think a better question might be, what is he?'

'Okay, I'll bite,' Helen said. 'What is a Danton Rhodes?'

'For starters, he's a man twice her age,' Annie said. 'Multi marriages in his past, each of them, of course, properly ended in divorce. After he had gone through whatever money his wives had.'

'He doesn't sound exactly savory,' Jake said.

'He's not,' Annie said, fairly spitting the words out. 'He's an overgrown playboy, a letch. I can't imagine . . . well, he is good looking, I'll give him that, and a smooth talker. He's exactly the sort of man a girl would be turned on to. A woman wouldn't, but a girl might.'

Jake thought for a moment. 'But, if your intuitions are correct, then the person with the best motive for harming Lois would be your father,' he said.

'Or Dee,' Helen said.

★   ★   ★

Mrs. Ricketts, whose night off it was, had declared for all to hear that she would go to a movie. 'A double feature,' she made sure everyone knew. 'There's one at the Strand that sounds interesting,' she added for emphasis. '*A Couple of Comedies.*'

Of course, Ricketts had no intention of actually going to a movie. In fact, the double feature playing at the Strand consisted of two movies both of which she had already seen twice; in case anyone later asked her about the films, she could tell them about either in detail.

When she came down to work earlier,

she had brought her white uniform with her in a plastic bag: white pants and a matching tunic, which in fact she rarely wore for her job, because it seemed to show every speck of dirt. For which reason, she waited until she was ready to leave for 'the movies' before she changed into the white outfit.

She wore her black coat over the white uniform when she left by the kitchen door, just in case anyone saw her leave, and although it was a warm night and the coat was a bit heavy for the weather, she waited until she had reached the hospital and was in the ladies' room there, before she took it off.

After that it was simply a matter of watching for the right opportunity to arise, but that bothered her not at all. She was used to waiting on the pleasure of the family she served, and in any event, she was supposed to be watching a double feature at the movie theater, so it would not do at all for her to arrive home too early.

Her visit here earlier with the family had given her an opportunity to check things out. Most of the nurses, she had observed, wore printed tops for their uniforms, but invariably their pants were white, as hers were, and her white tunic did not look all that unusual.

It was nine o'clock, or a little after, when she arrived at the hospital, and nearly midnight before she saw that the time was right for what she had planned. She left her coat and purse in a linen closet, where she hoped no one would accidentally discover them, and when she went out into the corridors, she found, as she had suspected, that no one paid her the slightest bit of attention. She looked, in fact, little different from any number of nurses who hurried past her.

From that earlier visit she already knew Lois Carter's room number but she did not go directly to that room. She went by a roundabout route, to be safe, up and down corridors and even taking the elevator down a floor and back up, smiling and nodding at an orderly who shared the elevator as if she might know him.

When she finally got to Lois's room, it was nearly one in the morning. As she had anticipated, no one was there except for the patient herself. To be sure, there were nurses just down the hall, at their station, but none of them had any reason to suspect anything was amiss with this patient.

Inside the room, dark but not completely so, Ricketts was disappointed to discover there was no way to lock the door from inside, but that she shrugged off as a minor inconvenience. She would just have to trust to her luck. So far it had gone very much her way.

She knew hospitals. She had worked in one for a brief time, albeit as a cleaning lady. Lois might be, and probably was, wired to machines which would alert the nurses at the station if there was any problem with the patient. But Meredith General was only a small community hospital, not much more than a clinic, really.

She felt confident that its methods and its equipment were almost certainly less sophisticated. There were cords attached to the sleeping woman, to be sure. Whether they were likely to set off alarms, she had no idea. But there again, she was prepared to trust to luck, which certainly seemed to be going her way.

And Lois Carter had been in a coma since she had arrived the night before. The doctors planned to perform surgery on her at seven o'clock in the morning, to look for brain damage, which meant the nursing staff would begin to prepare her for the surgery around five. In the meantime, it was more than likely they just supposed she would simply continue the deep slumber into which she had fallen. These nurses had many patients, most of them requiring more care than someone in a coma. Human nature was human nature. Ricketts doubted that Lois Carter was getting more than token attention from the nursing staff. It was how she would handle the case, and in most things, she thought that what she did was pretty much the norm for others.

Mrs. Ricketts had brought with her a large plastic bag, folded over and over so that it would fit into the deep pocket of her tunic. She took it out now and unfolded it, and went to the side of the bed.

This was the only part of which she was uncertain. Lois was attached to a variety of lines and tubes. She had to remove those that led to her mouth and nostrils. She held her breath as she did so, and stood for several long minutes waiting and listening.

After the wall clock had told her five minutes had elapsed, she began to breath more easily again. No one had come to investigate. Either no alarm had sounded, or the nurses were busy with other patients. Or perhaps they were just away from their station. She rather cynically suspected the latter to be the case. No one did more than they had to, in her opinion, in a hospital or at any other job. She certainly did not, and she doubted anyone else did either.

Confident now that she was in no danger of being detected, she lifted Lois's head from its pillow, and slipped the plastic bag over it, carefully tucking the end under her chin. After which, there was nothing for her to do but take a seat in the chair against the wall, and wait.

After about twenty minutes, she thought

she heard a death rattle from the bed. Nevertheless, to be safe, she waited the full half hour she had allotted for this step before tiptoeing carefully back to the bedside.

Yes, Lois was dead. Her eyes were open, but unseeing. To be extra sure, Ricketts checked carefully for a pulse, following the directions she had gotten from a book at the library. She found none. She carefully removed the plastic bag from off Lois's head and folding it, returned it to the pocket of her tunic. On the way home, she would shred it, and scatter the pieces as she went, so no one would ever even suspect its existence.

Something, however, had finally aroused the nurses at the station down the hall. A trio of them suddenly rushed into the room. But Ricketts had heard their hurried steps approaching at a run down the hall, and when they flung the door open, she was standing behind it.

For the moment, their attention was all on the patient on the bed. Ricketts slipped from behind the door and from the room, still unobserved. She retrieved her coat and purse where she had left them, and hurried from the hospital, noticed by no one. Just as she had supposed.

There was no longer any danger of Lois waking and telling anyone the story of what had really happened to her. Dee was safe.

★ ★ ★

Back at the house in Burbank, Gavin was awake, lying in bed, staring at the ceiling. From the floor beside him he heard the gentle snoring of the two sleeping there.

What a mess he had made of things. All of it, really, his whole life. Well, maybe only since he had met Dee. He could scarcely remember what his life had been like before that. It was as if some curtain had dropped down from above and blocked off his view of everything that had preceded it.

He had been in the military, the Marine Corps. But everything had become so muddled in his mind that he was only sure of that because he remembered clearly that he had been in his Marine uniform the night he met her. In uniform, and in the company of some friends from his base, Camp Pendleton. They had come up to the city together on the bus and they were in uniform, too, just as he was.

So, yes, at some point in time, he must have joined the military — the Corps, as they generally referred to it. In fact, if he worked at it, he could even remember enlisting, back in Kansas. But why he had done so, he could not imagine now. So far as he could recall, there hadn't been any other Marines in the family, no one whose example he was following.

Or, and this had occurred to him more than once, maybe you just forgot the stuff you didn't want to be there in the first place. Maybe the reason he could not remember his earlier life was because he did not want it to be whatever it had been. How could he say, when he couldn't remember it?

He did remember that he had met Dee at a bar in Hollywood, although she was adamant about not sharing that bit of information with her family.

'As far as they are concerned, I never

drink,' she explained. 'And I would like to keep it that way. I always say, what people don't know can't hurt them.'

He thought she was pretty. Not, in fact, the prettiest girl he had ever seen, but she was certainly pretty enough to catch all their eyes, him and his Marine Corps buddies. More than that, though, she had something, something he had never encountered before, and for which he really had no name: a spirit, sort of.

Or, it was more like a conviction, he supposed. Certainly she believed that she was the prettiest girl in the world, and by the time they had shared a drink, he was inclined to believe it too, if only because she herself was so certain of it.

He had heard before about people bewitching others. He had always thought it just a figure of speech. But after he met Dee, especially later, when he looked back upon their meeting, he had begun to think that maybe she had, literally, bewitched him.

The friends with him had, to a man, had suggestions to offer about what they would like to do with the pretty girl sitting alone at the bar. None of them had mentioned 'making love.'

Except, he had. He had actually said that to her, when she had asked him point blank what he had in mind, by buying her a drink. 'Making love,' he had said frankly.

Her eyes had gone wide with dismay. 'And we are not even married. You should be ashamed to suggest that to someone who is not even your wife. What kind of girl do you think I am, anyway?'

'Well, this is California. It takes some time to get married here, as I understand it.' He paused, and added, 'And I only have forty-eight hours.'

'Not in Mexico,' she said.

Which seemed to him awfully mysterious. 'Mexico?' he repeated, puzzled. 'What's Mexico got to do with anything?'

'It takes no time at all to get married in Mexico. You can do it in minutes. And it's only two or three hours down the coast highway to get there.'

'Are you suggesting . . . ?' he asked, and stopped. He thought he must surely be mistaken. He was, after all, just a country boy from back in Kansas, wearing a Marine uniform.

'I'm saying,' she said, giving him one of her 'looks,' 'if we left now, we could be there and be back by morning. A married couple.' She paused for a moment, and added, with a sly grin, 'And it's perfectly all right for married couples to make love, as you put it. That is, if you really wanted to. If you wanted to marry me, even.'

By this time, he did; of course he did, even though the idea had not entered his mind before she had suggested it. So it was goodbye to his buddies, who gave him some good-natured ribbing, and in no more than half an hour, he and Dee were speeding south on the Pacific Coast Highway, in her Mercedes but with him at the wheel.

They were headed for Mexico, a drive which took him right by Camp Pendleton. The quarrels — The Quarrel, as he thought of it later, because from then on it had never really stopped, hardly even abated — began on the drive back.

'But I thought,' she said, not much more than an hour after they had become

Mr. and Mrs. Gavin Rand at a little chapel in Tijuana, 'that you had some place to take me. Once we were married.'

'We could stop for the night,' he said, thrilled by the prospect and too shy to have suggested it without prompting. 'There's plenty of motels along here. We just have to pick one that isn't too expensive.'

'I wasn't thinking of a motel,' she said petulantly.

'Well, what were you thinking of?'

'A house. That's how married couples usually live, in a house,' she said. 'That's what I was expecting.'

'A house? But I live on a military base. On a marine's pay, too. Which isn't very much, if you didn't know.'

'I am not shacking up in a motel with you,' she said flatly. 'I don't care what you want.'

'Okay.' He had not really expected that to happen anyway. He honestly did not know what he had expected to happen. He had begun to feel like he was just along for the ride. This was her show.

'So where are we going, anyhow?' she

asked after a few miles of frosty silence.

'I was driving us to Burbank,' he said. 'Isn't that where you said you lived?'

'So your plan is to shack up at my house?' She could barely contain her disappointment. Her only reason for getting married was to escape the house in Burbank. And now she was headed back there, and with a husband she didn't want to boot. She felt trapped. Even more so than usual.

'Not for any length of time,' he said. 'I've got a forty-eight hour pass, remember. And twenty of them are already gone. By the time we reach Burbank, I figure I'll have less than one day left. Not even twenty-four hours. Not much of a honeymoon.'

Something to be grateful for, she thought, but did not say.

* * *

Her family took it better than he would have expected. They could not have been said to welcome him with open arms, but they did not slam the door in his face either. She could almost have thought her mother liked him, though what it really was, was that she thought this very serious young man might be the one to tame some of her daughter's wildness.

The only one of the family, in fact, who was openly cold and unfriendly toward him, was his wife. That first night — their only night together, as it turned out — she responded with equal passion to his passion, making him think that marriage had not been such a terrible idea after all, but when he left her in the morning to go back to the base, she barely opened her eyes, and when he said that it might be a month, maybe longer, before he could see her again, her only comment was a grunt.

In fact, although he wrote often and called almost every day, it was closer to three months later before he again was able to come to the house in Burbank. When he did, she informed him that she was pregnant.

'You are? That's great,' he said, delighted with the news.

She gave him a sour look. 'You think it is, do you? What's so great about it, I'd like you to tell me?' she said.

'I love kids,' he said, and after a moment, he asked somewhat hesitantly, 'Don't you?'

'I hate them,' she said vehemently. 'Utterly and absolutely hate them.'

'But why?' He was pretty sure he had never before even heard of anybody hating kids.

'Because everybody else has them.'

'So? What's so bad about being like everyone else?'

'Because I am not,' she said. 'I am not like everyone else. I'm not like anyone else, really. I'm special. You know I am, don't you?'

'Yes,' he admitted thoughtfully, 'I guess you are.' He had already learned that it was best not to disagree with his wife.

'No guess about it. But the thing is, though, people hate you when you're different, when you're special. They want you to be ordinary, same as them. Same as you, Gavin. That's why you think the way they do, because you're just one of them.'

'I suppose I am,' he admitted. 'I suppose that's why I fell in love with you.'

173

He tried to take hold of her then. He meant to embrace her, but to his surprise, she slapped his hands away.

'Don't touch me,' she cried, taking a step back from him. 'Don't you dare lay a hand on me, Gavin Rand. Don't you dare hit me.'

'Hit you? I wasn't going to hit you,' he said, alarmed. 'I was going to . . . '

But she never let him finish what he was trying to explain. She screamed, exactly as if he had struck her, and to his further horror, she began to claw at her own arms and at her face, until she was bleeding, screaming all the while.

'What's going on here?' That was her father, Douglas Carter, rushing down the stairs.

'I'm so sorry,' Gavin babbled. 'I'm so sorry.'

Only, he didn't quite grasp what it was that he felt sorry for. Something. But he never had been sure, then or since, exactly what.

★   ★   ★

174

Dee was at a party. Technically, she was there with Danton Rhodes, but since their arrival an hour or so earlier, she had successfully managed for the most part to ignore him. While she circulated, like a pink butterfly in the dress that Ricketts had ironed for her to wear, Danton sat in a chair against one wall, looking sulky and pretending he wasn't watching her full time out of the corner of his eye. Like most philanderers, Danton was of a jealous and possessive nature; sauce for the goose was certainly never, in his opinion, intended for the gander.

Of course, she knew he was watching. If she had thought for a single moment that he might not be, she would have concocted some way to correct that error on his part. She not only wanted men to have their eyes on her, she fully expected it. And woe betide the man who did not live up to her expectations.

She saw their hostess across the room. Betty Cameron was sitting in a large upholstered chair, holding her baby in her lap. Like The Madonna and Child, Dee thought jealously, although if asked she could not have named the painting to which she referred. She loathed babies, and their doting mothers, almost as much as she adored parties.

But there, she had always thought there was no use in avoiding things. Betty was someone with whom she had gone to school some years back, and the baby was the real reason for the party. The 'new baby,' as the invitation had described him, though in fact she was sure he must be six months old or more by now. And there was nothing for it; she was going to have to face up to mother and child sometime while she was here. Might as well get it over with, she thought bitterly, and sooner better than later.

She managed to get Betty's eye from across the room and, flashing her a delighted smile, began to work her way through the crowd to get to the chair where Betty sat. As she made her way, she tried to think how she was going to punish Betty, though if she had been asked for what exactly Betty deserved punishing, she could not have offered an explanation.

'Dee,' Betty greeted her with a friendly smile and seeming sincerity, though in fact the two of them had never been friends, as they both well knew. 'I'm so glad you could make it.'

'Wild horses couldn't have kept me away,' Dee said, with equal seeming sincerity. 'And this is little . . . Scott, is it?' she asked, lowering her face toward the baby's, her eyes conveying something of what she was actually feeling.

'Brad,' Betty corrected her.

Little Brad, who had been smiling at the nice people all evening, found something objectionable in the face now so very close to his own, particularly in the eyes that seemed to bore into his own. He tried to pull away, and when his mother's arms holding him close would not allow that, he screwed up his face instead, as if he had smelled something offensive.

Little beast, Dee thought, all the while smiling sweetly into the baby's face. She had noticed, as she came close, that little Brad's bare feet were protruding from beneath the blanket in which he was wrapped.

Now, knowing his mother could not possibly see her doing it, she took hold of one of his little toes and pinched it, hard.

For a moment baby Brad only looked puzzled. She pinched harder, digging her nails into the tender flesh, and he began to cry.

'Oh, dear,' Betty said, turning him toward her and patting his little bottom gently, 'I'm sorry. I have no idea why.'

'Oh, it's just babies,' Dee said graciously, drawing back. 'Sometimes there is no reason for them to cry. They just do, don't they? Maybe it's something he ate.'

'Oh, but no, we're so careful about his diet. Well, I am. You know how I am.'

'Indeed, I surely do.'

As long as she had known Betty, Betty had been on some diet or another. She dieted one week to lose weight, and the next to gain it. Or for her complexion, or to detoxify her liver. Or, and this Dee had always believed, just to have something to talk about. Some people were not clever at conversation, the way she was. She could always find something to chatter about, if only herself. More often than not, in fact, it was about herself. Who would not be interested in her? she often wondered.

'But usually he's so sweet-tempered,' Betty said. 'He's just the most pleasant-tempered little thing, so easy to get along with.'

'Like his father,' Dee said.

Betty, who had quarreled with her husband not half an hour before the first guest had arrived and was still sore enough to think him anything but easy to get along with, nodded. 'Well, of course. People do say so,' she said in a non-committal voice.

'He even looks like his father,' Dee added, feeling her way toward some sort of as yet undetermined malice.

'Do you think so?' Betty held the baby away from her bosom for a moment and regarded the little puckered face intently. 'Most people say he takes after me.'

Inspired, Dee suddenly screwed up her own face and gave a choked little cry. 'David's baby,' she said, in a strangled note.

'Well, yes, he is, of course,' Betty said, returning the baby to her lap and giving

Dee a funny look. 'Though I do like to think I had a little something to do with it too.' She laughed, although not with her eyes.

'I thought . . . at one time I was nearly certain of it, I was sure that I too would have a baby. His baby. Oh!' She clapped a hand to her mouth. 'I'm sorry. I didn't mean to mention that. I promised . . . Oh, never mind, it was just one of those slips of the tongue.'

'What are you trying to suggest?' Betty asked her coldly. 'And who did you promise?'

'No one, honest, I didn't mean a thing. I can't even think why I said such a thing.' Dee could not have looked more innocent, nor more apologetic.

'Well, why did you then?' Betty asked, not to be put off so easily.

Dee had spread her fingers over her face, but now she splayed them apart and peered out from between them, as if she were playing peek-a-boo with someone. 'You did know, did you not . . . surely David must have told you . . . '

'Told me what? Pray tell.' Betty's eyes were by this time flashing fire.

'Oh, nothing.' Dee waved her hand dismissively. 'If he didn't say anything . . . '

'Anything about what?' Betty's face was growing red with anger. 'I demand to know what you are talking about.'

'You did know, I suppose,' Dee stammered in a seeming agony of embarrassment, 'surely you must have known that I posed for him.'

'Posed for him? I don't understand, David is not that kind of painter. He paints landscapes. Barns, and streams, and . . . and things like that. He doesn't need models for the things he paints. And if he does, why, he goes out into the country.'

'Out in the woods. Yes. You're absolutely right. That's where we were.'

'Landscapes,' Betty emphasized. 'Those are his models. Not women. He doesn't need women for models.'

'I don't suppose any man does,' Dee agreed quickly. 'Not naked women, certainly. I told him that, the first time. I said, why on earth do you need me to take off my clothes? If you're just going to paint a waterfall? You see, you are entirely correct, there was a stream involved.'

Betty's eyes went wide. 'Are you telling me you posed for my husband with your clothes off?'

'Well, it's not like I am the only one,' Dee said indignantly. 'And what would you expect was going to happen, pray tell me, with people naked? And alone out in the woods? Of course I thought . . . well, when my period was late. What would you expect me to think?'

Betty was so angry now she could not even manage to get any words out. She sat sputtering, beads of spittle foam actually appearing at the corners of her mouth. And little Brad, perhaps because her grip on him had tightened, or maybe he only sensed the emotion, began to cry louder.

And Dee, staring at her, said, 'Oh, don't worry, it was just late. My period. It did come. A false alarm. So, there was really nothing to worry about. Nothing at all.'

And with that, she danced away. She twirled her way to where Danton was still sitting against the wall in his hard wooden chair. 'Up, Danton, up,' she said, reaching a hand out to him, 'it's time for us to go.'

His expression changed from bored to happy, and he jumped up so quickly that the chair fell, though neither of them noticed. He took her hand and started toward the door.

'Danton, I have decided, I want us to get married,' she said.

'But we are getting married,' he said. 'Next month. It's all arranged.'

'No, not then,' she said, 'Not that wedding. I mean now.'

'We can't get married now,' he said, laughing at her foolishness.

'Well, then, tomorrow, I mean. And stop laughing. I'm serious, damn you.'

★ ★ ★

Betty Cameron was still all but speechless when her husband David came to stand beside her chair.

'What's wrong with the baby?' he asked. 'I heard him crying clear out in the kitchen.'

'He's fine now,' she said.

And he was, too. The moment Dee had waltzed away, perhaps because his mother's grip had loosened a bit, he had stopped crying. He looked up at his father and laughed with some merriment all his own, as filled with delight now as he had been only a moment before with terror.

Betty, too, slanted a look up at her husband. 'That girl,' she said.

'What girl?' He looked blankly down at her.

'The one in the pink dress. She was just here, talking to me.'

'I didn't see her. I was in the kitchen. Mixing drinks.'

'It was Dee. Dee Carter.'

'I don't know her,' he said, but his eyes went right to her. Even in a crowded room, the neon pink dress was hard to miss.

'She knows you. She says she posed for you.'

'What?' he looked disbelieving.

'Naked,' she added.

'That's ridiculous,' he said angrily. 'She must have been pulling your leg. I don't do pinups. I paint landscapes. You know that.'

'I do know,' she said.

But the damage had been done. She did not like Dee, she never had. And she had always known that Dee was a liar. She would say anything that popped into her head, and swear to it on a Bible.

But the poison was inside Betty now, and could never be gotten out again. Logic was no antidote to what had been injected into her.

'I swear to you, I've never seen that girl before,' he said. 'You believe me, don't you?'

She stared long and hard at the handsome man to whom she was married.

'Of course,' she said, but it was not true. She did not believe him. She knew on the instant that she would never fully believe him again.

Or love him.

★   ★   ★

Annie was sitting alone on the sofa in the front room. She wore a short nightgown and a full length peignoir over it. Everyone else was abed except Ricketts, who had not yet come home from her movies, and Dee, who was at a party.

Earlier, Annie had peeked out the front

and back doors, and seen the guards still at each corner of the house. They were there to see that no one got in, but the problem was, they also effectively stopped anyone from getting out.

She had thought long and hard about how to get Gavin Rand out of here. She had even considered climbing out a window. There was a big tree just beyond the window of her room. But the guards outside would surely hear a window being opened, or see the leaves and branches of a tree shaking, and not only might they shoot Gavin as he tried to climb out, they were just as likely to shoot her as well.

So, without help, the chances of getting their secret roomie out of here were slim, as she saw it.

She heard a noise behind her, and looked to see Gavin standing in the doorway to the kitchen. He was wearing briefs, military green boxers, and nothing else. It occurred to her for the first time that he was actually a very good looking man.

At the same time, though, there seemed to be something wrong with him. His complexion looked waxy, unreal. She thought about that cough of his. He must be sick. Sicker than any of them had realized before now. Or was she only transferring her own unhappiness to this young man watching her so earnestly from across the room?

'I woke up and Jake and Helen were sleeping on the floor,' he said. 'It suddenly didn't seem right to me, me in their bed and them on the floor.'

'It was what they wanted,' she said. 'Besides, you shouldn't be out here. Ricketts could come home at any minute and find you, or Dee for that matter.'

'Maybe it's time I faced Dee,' he said. 'I can't keep hiding from her forever. These last couple of days, they've been bearing down on me, like a freight train heading for a man with his foot caught in the tracks. Anyway, there's something I learned while I was at that hospital. You have to take responsibility for things, face up to them. I don't care what they do to me. Besides, I have some money. I thought if maybe I gave it to Dee, she would agree to letting me take my son back.'

'Do you really think you can raise a kid all on your own?' she asked.

He blushed. 'No, I wouldn't even try,' he said. 'But I know someone who could. Someone who would take good care of him. That's really what I had in mind.'

She did not ask who he meant; it was really none of her business. 'You said you had some money. How much?' she asked instead.

'Fifty dollars,' he said. 'Almost sixty.'

She did not have the heart to tell him that a pittance like that was unlikely to influence Dee very much. Dee had never suffered for lack of money, her father had seen to that, and all too soon she was going to have a lot more of it. Way more than sixty dollars, certainly

'I doubt she would agree to that, knowing Dee. But it isn't just about you anymore, is it? Or your son either.'

'Why do you say that?'

'What do you think they would do to me if they knew I had been hiding you here all this time? Not to mention Jake and Helen?'

'I don't know. What?'

'They would probably arrest all three of us for harboring a fugitive. Is that what you want to see happen?'

'I hadn't thought of that.' He looked crestfallen. 'I guess I've really messed things up, haven't I?'

'Don't worry about it. So far we've got everything under control.'

'So, what do you want me to do?' He gave her an abject look.

'The way I see it you'll have to stay put at least for a little longer. I'm trying to think of some way to get you out of here without getting any of us shot. Oh, a car.' She looked frantically toward the front door. A vehicle had just pulled up in the gravel outside. A moment later, she heard a car door slam. 'Go, hurry.'

Gavin turned back toward the kitchen, but she said, quickly, 'No, not that way. If it's Ricketts, she'll come in through the kitchen. You could run smack dab into her.'

He looked around. 'Where can I go, then?'

She had to think. 'It'll have to be my room,' she said after a moment. 'Quick, up the stairs, it's the second door on the right. Wait there. I'll come up as soon as I can. Are you hungry?'

He paused halfway up the stairs. 'A little,' he admitted sheepishly.

'I'll bring you something, as soon as I can. Hurry, now, and don't slam the door.'

He went. A few seconds later her bedroom door closed softly. She scowled up the stairs after him. He looked unhappy. Worse, he looked defeated. But what more could she do than what she was already doing?

She heard voices from outside. Dee and Danton Rhodes, it sounded like, and they were quarreling.

The couple outside brought the quarrel inside with them. They failed to see Annie, sitting as still as a mouse on the sofa.

'We don't have to have a big wedding,' Dee said as they came down the steps from the foyer, 'Or that honeymoon in Paris, for that matter.'

'I thought you had your heart set on them,' Rhodes said.

'Ricketts does. I don't.'

'Well, you're right, she would probably

be disappointed if we just eloped.'

'Which as far as I am concerned is a good argument for eloping.' Dee glanced over her shoulder at him and saw his look of surprise. 'What? You think I want her trailing along with us forever. What do you think I want to get away from? What's the good of getting away, of getting married at all, if I am going to take everything with me?'

'But, I thought . . . well, aren't you very close, the two of you?'

'She certainly thinks so. It's a bore, if you ask me. She's worse than my mother was. Sometimes I feel like I can't even breathe, the way she hovers over me.'

'I never knew you felt that way.'

'Why should you? Oh, never mind about her. It's our wedding I'm thinking of. I don't see why we can't just run away. If we started out tonight, we would be in Mexico by morning. Nobody cares about anything down there. We could find one of those little chapels, it would all be over in minutes, and we could come back a married couple.'

Danton was thinking back to the

previous night, to Dee's assault on the hapless Lois. Most especially, he was thinking of Ricketts' threat to see him arrested as a party to the attack. Could Dee handle her? The last thing he wanted was to get himself sent to prison.

'Of course, I'll do whatever you say,' he said, stalling for time. 'But I don't think we should decide just this minute. We're not in that big a rush, are we?'

'Aren't we? Maybe you don't even want to marry me,' Dee said, striking a petulant pose. 'Is that it?'

'Don't be silly,' he said.

'The way you were acting with Lois . . . '

'Lois who?' he asked.

The talking stopped for a few minutes.

Oh, no, not now, Annie thought angrily. It was one thing to overhear a quarrel, but she was not going to sit here on the sofa a silent partner to their canoodling.

'Hello,' she said loudly. She sat forward and turned toward the couple at the foot of the steps. Just as she had thought from the silence, they were kissing.

Dee snapped her head around, her eyes

wide and angry. 'You,' she cried. 'What are you doing here?'

'Hello?' Annie said. 'I live here. Remember?'

'Why aren't you in bed? Go to bed, this instant,' Dee said imperiously.

'And what if I don't want to go to bed?' Annie asked. 'I don't take orders from you, Dee. I'll sit in this room as long as I like, thank you very much.'

'You're just spying on me, is all,' Dee said. 'Why? You're horrible. What business is it of yours what I do?'

'Absolutely none. And as a matter of fact, I was here first. So if you don't like it, you can just lump it.'

For an answer, Dee suddenly began to scream. Like a banshee. She threw her head back and shrieked, over and over, as if she was in unbearable pain.

The kitchen door flew open and Ricketts dashed in, her black coat flying behind her like a cloak. Annie was surprised to see her. Even more surprised to see that that under the black coat she wore a white uniform. She had never seen the housekeeper in white before.

'What is it, my darling?' Ricketts cried. What have they done to you?'

At almost the same moment, a sleepy-eyed Doug came down the stairs in pajamas and a bathrobe. He held the handgun in one hand, and rubbed at his eyes with the other.

'What's going on down here?' he asked. 'What's all the racket?'

'It's Annie,' Dee cried, pointing an accusing finger at her sibling. 'She's being mean to me.'

'Annie, for Pete's sake, what are you doing to your sister?' Doug demanded, turning on the younger girl.

'Never mind,' Ricketts said, shedding the black coat and tossing it over a chair, 'I'll take care of her.' She gave Annie a dark look and ran to where Dee was standing, seizing her in a gruff embrace, 'There, there, lambkin, you mustn't upset yourself so.'

'Oh, Ricky, I'm so unhappy,' Dee sobbed, dropping her head on the white uniformed shoulder.

Ricketts looks like a nurse, Annie thought. More like a nurse than a housekeeper. But then what Dee had said only a minute or so earlier popped into her mind, about wanting to get away from Ricketts. And now she was sobbing in Ricketts' arms like a frightened child.

What if Dee was only playing with Ricketts as if she were a doll? And when she tired of the doll, what then?

But wasn't that what her sister had done with Gavin as well. They had run off together, to Mexico, in fact, the same as Dee had suggested to Danton, and they had come back a married couple, to the quiet dismay of most of the family. But she had gotten tired of him, too, and very quickly. In time she got tired of everybody.

'Annie, what is the matter with you?' Doug demanded. 'And what are you doing up anyway? Go to bed.'

'I will,' Annie said, knowing when she was outnumbered. 'But I'm going to get myself a snack first. That's really what I came down for, to be honest. Some milk and cookies. I trust nobody minds. I can pay for them, if it's necessary.' She shot a hostile look around the room, but no one seemed even to be looking at her. As usual, everyone's attention was on Dee.

'I think I should go,' Danton said.

'Yes, do, why don't you?' Ricketts said over Dee's blonde head.

'I'll see you in the morning, Dee,' he said.

'I'll be packed,' she said without lifting her face from Ricketts' sturdy shoulder.

'Well.' He hesitated, casting an uneasy glance at Ricketts. 'We'll talk.'

'We have talked,' Dee said. 'And talked and talked.'

'Not enough, I don't think,' he said, and hurried up the steps to the foyer before she could say anything more. In another moment the front door had closed behind him.

'There, now, lamb, let's get you up to bed,' Ricketts said.

'I was hoping for a good night's sleep,' Doug said peevishly. 'Does anyone remember that I have to be up early to go to the hospital? Oh,' he looked down at the gun in his hands as if he had never seen it before. 'I guess I won't need to take this with me.'

He dropped it back into the drawer of the credenza. 'Now, if nobody minds terribly,' he said peevishly, 'I'm going back to bed. Maybe this time I'll be allowed to sleep.' He started back up the stairs.

Ricketts almost told him that it didn't matter, that he wouldn't be needed at the hospital in the morning, but she caught herself in time.

She wasn't supposed to know what had happened there.

13

Doug had scarcely disappeared from view up the stairs than the phone rang. Dee, standing almost beside it, answered.

'No, he's in bed, asleep,' she told whoever was calling. 'I can take a message for him, though. Yes, of course I'll see that he gets it.' She listened for a minute. 'Wait, say that again.' She paused. 'You're sure? Yes, I'll tell him.' She hung up and stood for a moment looking shocked.

'What is it, love,' a concerned Ricketts asked beside her.

Dee gave her a blank look. For a moment she seemed unable to speak. Finally, she blurted out, 'That was the hospital. They told me Lois is dead.'

'Yes, I know,' Ricketts said in a voice devoid of expression.

Dee gave her a puzzled look. 'But, how could you already know that? They just called to tell us.' Her eyes went wide. 'Oh, Lord, please don't tell me, you didn't, you had nothing to do with it. Did you?'

'I had to do it,' Ricketts said in an intense whisper. 'Don't look at me like that, lamby. And for Heaven's sake, lower your voice. No one else needs to know anything about this.'

'But, you . . . you . . . ' Dee stammered. 'What did you do? Why?'

'I told you why. It had to be done, that's why,' Ricketts said in a hoarse kind of whisper. 'Think, will you, in the name of Heaven? If she woke up, she could tell everyone what really happened here last night. The only way I could keep you safe was to be sure she never woke up. Now, you know what, and why. And there's no need for you to know how. Let's just forget all about it, why don't we? And what was that conversation with Mr. Rhodes, by the way, just before he left. That business about packing?'

'We're going to elope,' Dee said with a bright smile, her stepmother completely forgotten for the moment. 'We're running off to Mexico in the morning. We'll get married there.'

'Don't be a fool,' Ricketts said sharply,

and then more gently, 'You can't get married now anyway, don't you see? With your stepmother just now dead. How would it look? Not good, I should say. What would people think, you running off to get married just after your stepmother dies?'

Dee gave her head a toss. 'I don't care what anyone thinks.'

'You should. Besides, we want the big wedding, don't we?' Ricketts went on in a wheedling tone. 'All those presents and people congratulating you. Just think how it would be. You'd be the center of everyone's attention.'

'I am anyway. I always am. You know it's true.'

Ricketts ignored that. 'And afterward, Paris,' she went on in the same coaxing murmur. 'I'll go with you, my lamb, to take care of everything.' And get rid of that fool husband in due time, she thought but did not say aloud. Then it would be just the two of them, just her and her little girl, and all that money. And no stupid males underfoot.

Dee remembered Lois then, and what

Ricketts had confessed to her. She gave a wail and pulled away from the house-keeper. 'You shouldn't have done it.'

'It had to be done, I tell you,' Ricketts said sharply, angrily.

'You're too stupid to get away with something like that. They'll know. They'll catch you.'

'Catch us, you mean,' Ricketts fairly hissed. 'I wasn't the one who beat the poor woman unconscious last night. Do try to keep that in mind, won't you?'

'Oh.' Dee groaned, but softly. 'You're horrible. I hate you.' She spun away from the woman, tossing her blonde hair about in a frenzy. She went as far as the sofa and sank down in a heap upon its cushions.

Ricketts started to go after her, and stopped herself. Maybe it would be better to leave her little girl alone for a bit, she thought. Give her time to ponder on their situation. Once she had thought about it, she would see the necessity of what had been done. She would be grateful then.

'I'll get you a glass of water,' she said.

She almost ran into Annie, coming

from the kitchen. Annie was carrying a large bowl of soup in both hands, walking carefully so as not to spill it.

'Cookies and milk?' Ricketts said, raising an eyebrow.

'I found some chicken soup in the fridge,' Annie said. 'I decided that sounded better.'

'Maybe I was saving that for my own lunch,' Ricketts said. 'Did you even think of that?'

'Mrs. Ricketts, you do remember, do you not, that you work here?' Annie said sharply. 'I suspect my father paid for whatever went into this soup. If I want to eat it, I will. As for your lunch, I think I also saw some bologna in there. Make yourself a sandwich.' She went past the housekeeper, still carrying the bowl very carefully.

Mrs. Ricketts continued into the kitchen, calling Annie something under her breath that she would not have dared to say aloud.

Annie saw no sign of Dee in the front room, and supposed that she had gone up to her own room. She wondered idly about that ringing of the phone she had heard from the kitchen. It was an odd time of night for anyone to be calling. Who on earth might it have been?

Just at the moment, though, she had other things on her mind. She made her way slowly across the room and up the stairs.

Gavin, apparently lulled by the silence, had come out onto the landing. He looked, she thought worrisomely, like he was ready to bolt. 'Here,' Annie said, thrusting the bowl at him. 'And back inside, pronto.' She followed him into her bedroom.

She had left the windows open earlier and the breeze outside had set the curtains billowing, dancing like ghosts. They seemed to be trying to warn her of something.

Downstairs, Dee, still huddled on the sofa, had heard the exchange between Ricketts and Annie, which only made her smile. Was it possible, her sister was finally growing a backbone?

But the silence that followed was puzzling. She lifted her head just in time to see Annie hand the bowl to Gavin. A minute later, both of them had disappeared into Annie's room.

Dee laughed softly to herself. Oho. So that's how it is, is it, she thought?

★ ★ ★

'This soup is delicious,' Gavin said, tasting it. 'Or maybe I was just starving.'

'Eat it all. Every drop,' Annie said. 'I suppose I could go back down to the kitchen and get you a glass of milk.'

'That sounds good.'

'Only,' she hesitated, frowning. 'Ricketts is there. And probably Dee too. She was in the front room earlier, but she vanished from there. She might have gone to her room. Or by now, she could be in the kitchen with Ricketts.'

'In that case, forget the milk,' Gavin said. 'This will do just fine. And to be honest, now that I've finished it, I feel like going back to bed. I'm all sleepy again.'

'Then sleep,' she said. 'Your body is most likely trying to tell you something.'

'I think you're right,' he said. He was

sitting on the edge of the bed. He set the empty bowl on the nightstand and fell back on the bed's surface, yawning. 'You won't mind if I take a nap?'

'Not at all.'

He closed his eyes, and in what seemed no more than seconds, his breathing had deepened. A moment later, he began to snore softly.

Annie had been thinking about sleep herself. She was tired, more tired than she probably ought to be. She looked critically at the young man sleeping atop the bedcovers; in the very middle of the bed. Unless she wanted to get on very friendly terms with him, it was not going to be possible for her to sleep there too.

She decided that she would go for a walk instead. Maybe the night air would restore her energy. She turned out the lamp on the nightstand by the bed. The ceiling light was on a dimmer switch. She dialed it down to its lowest setting, until the room was suffused with no more than a faint glow.

She let herself out of the room, pausing in the doorway to canvas the room below.

There was no sign of Dee. She closed the bedroom door behind herself and hurried down the stairs, to the front door.

14

In the kitchen alone, Ricketts began to stew over Dee's attitude earlier. She was fearful of what the child might do when she was in the throes of anger. She might very well say the wrong thing to the wrong somebody, and get both of them into serious hot water.

Ricketts filled a glass with cold water from a pitcher in the refrigerator (no tap water for her little girl) and got one of her tranquilizers from the bottle in her purse, and was about to carry both with her, back into the front room when Dee showed up in the kitchen, looking utterly delighted with herself.

'Here you go, love,' Ricketts said, offering them to the smiling young woman.

Dee took the glass of water, drinking from it thirstily. 'My but it is a warm night,' she said. She looked suspiciously at the pill in Ricketts' hand. 'What's that?' she asked.

'Just one of my tranquilizers,' Ricketts said. 'It will help you to calm down.'

'I'm calm enough,' Dee said in a sulky tone.

'You won't be if that madman shows up,' Ricketts said. 'And he's likely to do just that, from what they say.'

'He's already here,' Dee said, and turned away from the offered pill.

'What? What do you mean?' Ricketts was aghast. She dropped the pill into her pocket.

'Just that. I mean, he is in the house already.'

'He can't be.' Ricketts gave her a suspicious look. 'What makes you say that?'

'I saw him.'

'But . . . but,' Rickets sputtered. 'That's not possible. Not with those armed guards outside. No one could get in past them.'

'Maybe he got in sooner, before they were posted outside,' Dee said with a smug smile. 'Maybe he's been here all the time. I'll bet nobody even thought of that.'

Ricketts looked doubtful, but not altogether incredulous. 'I suppose that is possible, but, I don't understand. Are you sure? You saw him? Where?'

'He's . . . ' Dee's face was turned away, so that Ricketts did not actually see the sly expression that crept over Dee's countenance just then. 'He's down in the cellar.'

'In the cellar? But how could you have seen him down there?'

Dee looked at her then with an expression of utter innocence. 'I didn't actually see him. I just said that. I don't even know why I said it. I heard him, though. It's the same thing, really.'

'Down in the cellar? Maybe what you heard was a mouse,' Ricketts suggested, looking amused.

'Not hardly. Not unless mice swear.'

'You heard him swearing?' Ricketts' amusement turned to alarm.

'Not loud. Under his breath, sort of. Like maybe he had run into something in the dark, or stubbed his toe. I don't know why. He just did.'

'What did he say?' Ricketts asked.

Dee huffed indignantly. 'He said, 'damn,' if you must know. I heard him clearly. And it was Gavin's voice, I'd swear to that. I'd know his voice anywhere, after what he did to me.'

'But, what were you doing in the cellar?'

'I wasn't in the cellar,' Dee said sharply. 'I was going to go down there, until I heard his voice. And of course, then I didn't go. I'm not crazy, you know, just because . . . '

'Why?' Ricketts interrupted her.

'Why? I just told you why. I heard Gavin down there. I wouldn't have gone down there after I heard him.'

'No, I meant, why would you be going down into the cellar in the first place?'

Dee took a moment to consider her answer. 'Mother, my real mother, I mean, had some blackberry jam put up, ages ago, and I remembered it fondly. It used to be on the shelf down there, and while you were out earlier, I had a fancy for some. So I opened the door and was about to go down to see if I could find it, and I heard him swear. Well, of course, then I closed the door again and locked it. So he couldn't get out.'

'Of course. Good girl. How clever of you. When the police chief comes by next time, we'll tell him, and let him catch the madman.'

'No,' Dee said. 'We can't do it that way.'

'Why ever not?' Ricketts asked. 'It's the sensible thing to do, seems like to me'

'But it's the same as Lois, isn't it? If he talks to them, he'll tell them all sorts of things about me. Wicked things.'

'No one will believe him. He's a madman,' Ricketts said. 'No one listens to what crazy people have to say.'

'They might listen to him,' Dee said. 'And people might start to wonder. What if he tells them he was here all last night? Which means, he couldn't have been at the hospital.'

Ricketts thought about that for a moment. 'Yes, you're right,' she said. 'If he was locked in the cellar, he could not have harmed Lois. And if they start wondering who did . . . '

'But if he were dead, he couldn't say

anything, could he?' The sly expression slid down over her face again. 'That's what you said about Lois, isn't it?'

'Well, yes, sort of,' Ricketts conceded. 'But, this is different. Very different. Lois was unconscious. And a woman. But your ex-husband is a man, a young one, probably strong, too. He was in the army, wasn't he?'

'The Marine Corps.'

'The same thing. And from what you say, he's entirely conscious. Unless he was swearing in his sleep, which seems unlikely. I doubt we could overpower him, even with two of us about it.'

'Wait.' Dee ran from the kitchen into the living room, to the credenza against the wall. She opened the top drawer and found the handgun lying there, and took it back to the kitchen with her. 'There is this. I saw Daddy put it in the drawer in the credenza a little while ago.'

'A gun?' Ricketts stared at it as if Dee were holding a venomous snake in her hand. 'But I've never used one. I'm not sure I would even know how.'

'It's easy. You just point it and pull the

trigger. I shouldn't think it would be all that different from — well, whatever you did before.' She gave the housekeeper an ingenuous look.

'No, I suppose that's true.' Ricketts took the gun from her, holding it with both hands and looking worriedly at it. 'And you're right, it does change things. He's in the cellar, you said?'

'Yes. Here, follow me.' Dee led the way through the kitchen, to the cellar door, Ricketts plodding without enthusiasm after her. The key was in the lock. Dee turned it and opened the door a crack. Standing just behind her, Ricketts took a deep breath and stepped forward.

'You stay here,' she said in a whisper. 'If he's down there, I mean to shoot him right off. No one will blame us. Two women, a madman in the cellar. They'll make heroes of us.'

'Don't give him any chance to jump you,' Dee said, whispering as well. 'Shoot the minute you set eyes on him.'

'I will.' Ricketts held the gun in front of her, still clasping it in both hands, and took a deep breath. She nodded for Dee to open the door. Dee swung it wide, into the kitchen. Ricketts stepped through, onto the landing.

She paused there to take another deep breath. This was a far different thing from killing someone who was already unconscious. Who knew what perils might be waiting for her in the darkness below?

'Hello?' she called aloud. It would be much easier if Gavin just came to the foot of the stairs. She could shoot him from where she was, with hardly any chance of missing him, she thought, and no risk to be taken on her part.

There was neither sound nor motion from below, however. She looked back at Dee. 'You're sure he's down there?' she asked.

'Positive. Here, give me the gun.'

'But I can't go down there unarmed,' Ricketts said in a fierce whisper.

'You're not going to. We just want him to come to the foot of the stairs, where he'll see you standing up here. Wait.' She spun back into the kitchen to turn off the light.

'There,' she said. 'Now all he'll see is

you at the top of the stairs. He won't see me standing behind you. Not until I shoot him. Which I'll do as soon as he comes to the foot of the stairs. Give me the gun.' She held her hand out.

Ricketts gave her the gun, reluctantly. 'Just be sure you don't shoot me,' she said.

'I won't. When I yell, you duck down.'

'I can't duck. I've got a bad back.'

'Then just drop to the floor. Like you have fainted. Go on, now, step onto the first stair.'

Ricketts stepped down onto the first step, and said again, 'Hello?'

'Gavin!' Dee yelled past her. 'We know you're down there. Come out with your hands up.'

'Well, if he was asleep, that ought to wake him up,' Ricketts said. She went down another step.

As she did so, Dee put the flat of her hand between Ricketts' shoulder blades, and shoved, hard. Ricketts gave a low, smothered cry, and tumbled downward, head first. By the time she reached the bottom step, she was already unconscious.

Dee did not wait for that to happen, however. The moment Ricketts began to tumble, she slammed the cellar door shut and turned the key in the lock. She gave a little laugh and danced around in a circle, before thinking to remove the key from the lock and dropping it into the pocket of her skirt. Just in case anyone else thought of checking the cellar.

Then, still holding the gun, she ran, giggling, out of the kitchen, across the front room, and up the stairs, to her own bedroom.

She closed the door and leaned breathlessly against it. So much, she told herself, for a honeymoon in Paris with Ricketts tagging along.

As for Danton Rhodes, he would do as he was told. He always did, though sometimes he liked to put up an argument. In the end, though, he knew perfectly well who was running things.

Now there was only her ex-husband to deal with.

And her sister Annie, of course.

15

'He's gone,' Jake said.

'Huh?' Helen, still curled up in the sleeping bag on the floor, opened one eye. 'Who's gone?' she asked in a sleepy voice.

'Gavin. Your cousin.'

'Cousin-in-law, I think he'd be.' Helen sat up, suddenly awake. 'Gavin? What do you mean, he's gone?'

'Gone.' Jake waved a hand at the empty bed, 'Like, he's not here.'

'But . . . he can't be gone.' Helen got hurriedly to her feet, kicking the sleeping bag away where it wanted to cling to one foot, and looked at the empty bed. 'You're right,' she said. 'He's not here.'

'I said that.' Jake spread his hands. 'So, what do we do about it?'

'First, we find Annie. She was keeping an eye on things.'

They showered, together, which involved some play time, and by six they were out in the kitchen, where they found Annie, arranging some dishes on a tray.

'Grannie likes her breakfast served to her in bed,' she said, putting some freshly buttered toast on a small plate, 'And Ricketts seems to have disappeared. So, I guess I'm maid for the day.'

'She's not the only one who's disappeared,' Helen said. 'Gavin is gone too.'

'Gavin?' Annie glanced around the room but the three of them were definitely alone. Nevertheless, she dropped her voice to a whisper. 'He hasn't gone all that far. He's upstairs, in my bedroom. Second door on the right.'

'And this is because . . . ?' Jake raised an eyebrow.

'He was all prepared last night to give himself up, if you want to know. I think he's very depressed.'

'I'm not surprised,' Helen said, thinking about what Mrs. Hurst had told them back in Santa Monica.

'Oh, I talked him out of giving himself up, but by the time he was ready to go back to bed, Ricketts was due home, and I was afraid they might run into one another here in the kitchen, so I sent him up to my room. I thought it would be safer all around.'

'Giving himself up?' Helen was stunned. 'Why did he want to do that?'

'He said maybe it was time he faced up to Dee. Faced his responsibility, is how he put it.'

'Maybe he thought it just didn't matter,' Jake said.

'That's an odd way to look at it,' Annie said. 'Why wouldn't it matter?'

Helen wasn't sure, however, it was entirely kosher to share something that had been blurted out to them by a distraught mistress who probably hadn't intended it to become common knowledge. Certainly Gavin, who hadn't mentioned his illness to them, hadn't intended that to happen.

'Faced his responsibility?' Helen said, hearkening back to what Annie had said. 'That would be fine, assuming everyone else did the same.'

'But they usually don't,' Jake said.

'Exactly,' Helen agreed. 'Dee won't, that's for sure. She does these things, and she never intends them to go bad, but they do, because no matter how awful they are, she just can't help herself using them against people. They are her weapons. And weapons are meant to be deployed, whatever excuses people give themselves.'

'That does sound like Dee,' Annie said. She stifled a big yawn.

'Bad sleep?' Jake asked.

'No sleep,' Annie said. 'I've got someone in my bed, remember?'

'He's kind of cute, don't you think?' Helen said with a wink.

'Not that cute. Look, just so you know, there's a motel down the street. Nothing fancy but it's clean and comfortable. I've had friends stay there before. As soon as I've taken Granny her breakfast, I'm going to stroll down there and get a room. Oh, don't worry, I'll still be in and out of here, so no one will know. But it will give me some place to sleep until we figure out what to do about Gavin. Which, I hope, will be soon.'

The coffee pot was making noises, and by the time Helen had toasted some bread, the coffee was ready. She poured cups for herself and Jake, and Annie filled a cup for her grandmother, set it on the tray and took it with her out of the kitchen. As she went out, Police Chief Tyler was coming in. He helped himself to coffee and sat down with Jake and Helen at the little breakfast nook.

'So, my investigation tells me that you,' he pointed at Jake, 'used to be with the San Francisco Police Department,' he started the conversation.

'Used to be is right,' Jake said.

'Wait, are you saying,' Helen asked indignantly, 'you had us investigated?'

'I did, yes,' Tyler said.

'That sounds, I don't know, kind of sneaky,' Helen said.

'I'm a policeman,' Tyler snapped. 'That's what I do. I investigate: things, people, whatever arouses my curiosity. Which, to be honest, you two did.' He narrowed his eyes. 'Are you guys on some kind of a case at present? Why did you come here, anyway? Burbank is really sort of a backwater.'

'In case you've forgotten, these people are my family,' Helen said. 'I came for a visit. I don't see anything suspicious in that.'

'I said curiosity, not suspicion.' Tyler turned his attention to Jake. 'You were a ranger,' he said, almost as if he were making an accusation.

'I spent some time in the Army, yes,' Jake conceded.

'You were awarded a silver star,' Tyler said. 'Weren't you?'

'They took a few shots at me. The North Vietnamese,' Jake said reluctantly. 'Where is this going, anyway?'

'To be frank with you,' Tyler said with a sigh, 'I have been thinking, a big city detective could be useful. You were on the homicide detail with the SFPD, I believe the report said. Is that right?'

'I was,' Jake said.

'This was after the Rangers.'

'Right,' Jake said.

'So what do you think of the situation here? Either of you have any thoughts?'

'Plenty of them. For starters, I think he didn't do it.' Helen said. 'Gavin Rand didn't beat Lois senseless, I mean.'

'What makes you so sure of that?' Tyler looked dubious.

'His doctor said he had been discharged

from that hospital. Ages ago. So he wasn't really an escapee, or a madman,' Jake said. 'Which is the way these people keep describing him. He sounds to me like he's completely harmless.'

'But as Dee said, doctors can make mistakes, same as anybody else,' the chief pointed out.

'Even policemen make mistakes,' Helen said.

Tyler allowed himself the ghost of a smile. 'That's true. We do. But in this instance, I do have a witness who puts him on the scene.'

'Dee,' Helen said with a disparaging snort.

'Yes, Dee. And Gavin Rand has a history of violence, at least against women. He attacked his wife once before.'

'Did he?' Helen said. 'That's what Dee says, but what if he says different?'

'Well, as far as that goes, so long as he remains missing, I have no idea what he might say. And even if he did say different, that's just his word against hers.'

'And hers is sacrosanct, I suppose,'

Helen said sarcastically.

Tyler gave her a considering look. 'Not necessarily,' he said. 'Look, I'll tell you what, the doctors are scheduled to operate on my sister this morning. Doug will be coming down soon, to go to the hospital, and I was planning on driving him there, so I can be there too. And once my sister is awake, we can ask her about what happened. Then we'll know the real story, won't we?'

'We?' Jake asked.

'I was going to suggest, why don't the two of you come with me? That way, you'll be there too when she comes out of the coma.'

'I'd like that,' Helen said.

'But I have to warn you,' Tyler added, 'you'll not be acting in any official capacity. You will be observers, and advisors, only, if you so choose. But this remains my case, period.'

'Fair enough,' Jake said, and Helen nodded.

'Why the sudden interest in us?' she asked.

'We don't have a lot of homicides in

Burbank,' Tyler said. 'How about we just leave it at that, okay?'

They followed him out of the kitchen. 'You never told me about the silver star,' Helen said to Jake in a whisper.

'Helen, it's just a piece of tin. Don't get excited,' Jake whispered back.

Tyler heard the exchange. Without slowing his steps or looking back, he said, 'The Silver Star is awarded for bravery in battle. And it's the third highest medal a man in the military can get.'

'I got some stiches,' Jake said, not looking at either of them. 'That's what it's about.'

'According to the report, they took something like thirty pieces of frag out of your back. Because you were protecting your fellow rangers. It says you damned near died from the loss of blood.'

Jake's response was a grunt that might have meant anything.

Typical, Helen was thinking. I couldn't just get an ordinary jerk, the same as every other girl lands at least once in her life. Oh, no, I had to get a modest jerk. Not to mention a heroic one.

But one with possibilities, she quickly added, and smiled at Jake. No use in pretending; she did love the big ape.

★   ★   ★

They learned, as soon as they had arrived at the small hospital in the Verdugo hills above Burbank, that Lois Carter was not going to tell them anything when she awakened, for the starkest of reasons: she would awaken never again.

'How did she die?' Jake asked.

'Asphyxiation, essentially.' The doctor turned to Doug. 'The nurse says she called your house last night to tell you.'

'Asphyxiation, how?' Jake persisted.

'Without getting too technical,' the doctor said, 'she died from lack of air in her lungs. As sometimes happens with people in a coma. Their brains forget to tell the lungs to breathe.' He again turned to address Doug. 'The nurse says she talked to someone who said she was your daughter, and who swore that she would tell you.'

All of them thought about that for a

moment; like dog poo on a sidewalk, everyone cautiously sidling around it, no one wanting to get too close.

'They must have talked to Annie, probably,' Doug said finally. 'And most likely, she just forgot.'

'It seems an odd thing to just forget,' Tyler said.

'Never mind that. I'm going to talk to my attorneys,' Doug said. 'This is criminal negligence on the part of the hospital.'

'You're right about the criminal part,' Jake said, standing just inside the door to the room, 'but it wasn't negligence, and it wasn't the hospital's doing.'

'What do you mean?' Tyler asked him. 'Are you suggesting that my sister's death was not the hospital's fault?' He gave Jake an appreciative glance. 'What makes you say that?' he asked

'Aside from a coma, there are three causes for asphyxiation,' Jake said. 'Strangulation, drowning and smothering. There are no bruises around her neck to suggest strangulation, and it's unlikely that she drowned lying in a hospital bed. So, she was smothered.'

'But there is, as the doctor says, the matter of her coma,' Tyler said.

'Look at her eyes,' Jake said. Lois's eyes were open wide, though unseeing. 'They're bloodshot, am I right?'

'They are, yes, even I can see that,' Doug said. He looked at Tyler. 'Does that mean something?'

'It means she was smothered,' Tyler said. He looked at the doctor. 'Am I right?'

The doctor leaned closer to the bed to look at Lois's eyes. 'Yes,' he said simply. 'It appears that way. There is petechial hemorrhaging.'

'What does that mean?' Helen asked.

The doctor aimed a finger at her eyes. 'Those pinpoint, reddish spots. You can see them if you look closely. They are caused by the pressure on blood vessels.'

'Which is to say, you did not look closely enough to start with,' Tyler said.

The doctor straightened and spread his hands in a gesture of defeat. 'That is true. She was in a coma. I just supposed . . . well, whatever I supposed, it seems I was mistaken.'

'Do you have a time of death?' Tyler asked.

'The monitors alerted the nurses about twelve thirty in the morning.'

'If she was smothered, shouldn't there have been an earlier warning?' Jake asked.

'You mean if the support systems were disabled?'

'If someone murdered her, they must have been. Wouldn't you say?'

The doctor looked at him darkly. 'Yes. If the support systems were disabled, there should have been a warning then.'

'Which the nurses may have missed.'

'Nurses are only human. And the patient had been in a coma since she had been brought in. They may have prioritized their patients.'

'Meaning,' Helen said, 'First attention would have gone to those most likely to respond to treatment?'

'Yes. But of course, if a monitor signaled that someone was in really critical shape . . . '

'In San Francisco,' Jake said, 'the Bureau looked on every case of a person smothered as suspicious and requiring further investigation.'

'By which I take it you mean an autopsy,' Tyler said.

'Oh, dear, I'm not sure how we feel about that,' Doug said. 'The family, I mean.'

'I don't think it matters what the family thinks,' Tyler said. He looked at Jake. 'Am I right?'

'Right,' Jake said. And to Doug, 'California law requires an autopsy in any case where the coroner considers the death to be suspicious. And I think you'll find that in this case he does.'

'I would have to agree,' the doctor said. 'And I will tell him so.'

'Plus,' Jake added, 'I don't even need to wait for the results to come back. I can tell you now some of what he is going to find. She'll have high levels of carbon dioxide in her blood. That's typical of smothering cases. And most likely, particulates in her lungs and airways. From whatever was used to smother her. Plastic, maybe, or down from a pillow.'

'What are you trying to say?' Doug demanded.

'I'm not *trying* to say anything.' Jake said, 'I'm telling you flat out that this was no accident, and it was not carelessness on the part of the hospital staff.'

'What he is saying,' Tyler said, 'Is that your wife, my sister, was murdered. Smothered.'

'Obviously, by someone,' Helen added, 'who did not want her to wake up, ever again.'

'By that madman,' Doug said. 'It had to be Gavin Rand. Somehow he got to her in here.'

'That's ridiculous,' Helen said. 'Why would he want to kill her?'

'Who else would want to?' Doug said. 'For Pete's sake, of course it was him.'

Looking at Doug, listening to him, Helen thought that it was impossible to beat a river into submission. The best you could do was to go with its current; but she had to admit, at least to herself: she did not like the channel into which Doug's thoughts were flowing.

16

The grandmother, having had breakfast, was seated on the sofa in the parlor, and Annie was just about to go out the door when the group got back from the hospital.

'Lois is dead,' Doug said without preamble

'Oh, no,' Annie cried. 'How awful.'

'Awful is right,' Grannie said. 'The poor woman. Was it that crazy man?'

'Seems like it to me,' Doug said. 'But,' he turned his attention to Annie, 'Didn't you know?' he asked, bewildered.

'Me? But how could I?' She matched him in bewilderment.

'They said, at the hospital, they called here last night. The nurse said she talked to my daughter.'

'It wasn't me,' Annie said.

'Then it must have been Dee,' Helen said.

'I doubt that,' Doug said. 'But let's find out.'

'How?' Helen asked.

'That's easy,' Doug said. 'I'll ask her.' He went to the foot of the stairs and yelled up them, 'Dee, honey, come down here this minute. I need to ask you something.'

In a moment, Dee had appeared at the top of the stairs. 'What is it?'' she asked. "I'm busy."

'Doing what?' Annie asked, although she thought she already knew the answer.

'I'm packing if you want to know,' Dee said, and as quickly dismissed her sister from her mind. 'What was it, Daddy? What did you want?'

Doug was torn, wanting to know why she was packing, and wanting an answer to his question. The latter won out for the moment.

'They say at the hospital they called here last night to tell me Lois was dead, and that they talked to someone, a female obviously, who said she was my daughter.'

'It must have been Annie?' Dee said. 'Annie, did you talk to the hospital last night?'

'Not I!' Annie said. 'I didn't answer the

phone the whole night. But I heard it ring. I was in the kitchen at the time. You and Ricketts were in here, as I recall.'

'Then it was probably Ricketts who talked to them,' Dee said, unconcerned. 'Yes I seem to remember her talking to someone.'

'Whoever it was told the nurse she was my daughter,' Doug said.

'You know how Ricketts is, Daddy,' Dee said. 'She'll say anything.'

'Speaking of whom,' Annie said. 'Ricketts seems to have disappeared. Would you happen to know where she is, Dee?'

'How should I know?' Dee asked. 'I'm not the housekeeper's keeper.' She giggled at her own cleverness and, turning, went back into her own room.

'Well, I'm sure I don't know either,' Annie said, and started again for the door.

'Wait. Where are you going?' her father asked.

'Out,' she said. 'For a walk. I'm tired of feeling like I am a prisoner here.' She paused for a second or two as she passed Helen, just long enough to whisper, 'He's asleep. I left the overhead light on.' And with that, she was gone, out the front door.

'Oh, dear,' Grannie said. 'Should she be traipsing about outdoors by herself until we know what is happening around here?' She looked at Helen and then Jake. 'Maybe one of you ought to go with her.'

'You're right.' Jake said, and before Helen could object, he had gone out the door in Annie's wake. Helen followed, but more slowly.

'Well,' the old lady said, to no one in particular, 'It doesn't seem as if there is anything I can do down here. I guess I might as well go back to my room. Things are nice and quiet there. I can rest, at least.'

'I think I'll do the same,' Doug said. 'Tyler, you okay? You look kind of, I don't know, perplexed.'

'I am,' the police chief said. 'We still don't know what happened to Lois.'

'Maybe you don't, but I don't have any doubts,' Doug said. 'You mark my words, once we've got our hands on that loony, everything will become clear.'

He went up the stairs. Tyler stared after him for a minute, thinking. Then, with a sigh, he went out the front door. He found Helen on the front steps, staring off down the driveway.

'They've gone?' Tyler asked. It occurred to him just then why Helen was staring into the night. 'I've got my car,' he said. 'We could go after them, if you want. They can't have gone far.'

Helen, thinking about the motel room and why Annie had rented it, and of Gavin asleep upstairs in Annie's room, shook her head. The last thing she wanted was to get Tyler started wondering what was going on.

'No, they'll be fine,' she said.

'Suit yourself,' Tyler said. He shrugged. Who knew how women thought? He went down the steps to his cruiser, got in it, and drove away down the curving driveway.

Helen watched until the taillights had disappeared from sight. For a moment longer, she thought of that motel Annie had mentioned. But, heck, she didn't even know where it was. As for Annie and

Jake — well, she was sure nothing untoward was going to happen. Pretty sure, anyway.

A breeze had come up, making the Japanese maples stir and mutter among themselves. As she was going back inside, the wind tugged the door out of Helen's careless hand, and slammed it shut with a loud bang. At almost the same moment, Helen heard a sharp report from upstairs. Another door slamming, she wondered? The wind must be stronger than she had supposed.

She was halfway across the front room, on her way to her own bedroom in the rear, when the truth suddenly dawned on her: that had not been a door slamming. It had been a gunshot.

She raced back across the room and up the stairs, to the second door on the landing. She burst into Annie's room. It was dark. Hadn't Annie told her she had left the light on? She flicked the switch, bathing the room with a pale glow. She adjusted the dimmer switch, bringing the light up to its full luminescence.

At first, she thought the room was

empty. Certainly the bed was, although she was sure Annie had whispered that Gavin was sleeping in it. Or, no, she had simply said he was sleeping.

But sleeping on the floor? Because that was where she saw Gavin when her eyes went around the room a second time, lying on the floor between the bed and the door. And not, as she and Jake had done, in sleeping bags. He was just stretched out across the hard wooden floor, not even on the skimpy throw rug by the bed. It looked more as if he had gotten up from the bed, had started toward someone, or just toward the door, and then tripped and fallen.

Except, when she knelt, meaning to shake Gavin awake, Helen realized Gavin had not simply tripped and fallen. He had been shot, as evidenced by the blood Helen got on her hands when she tried to turn him over. Shot in the middle of his forehead.

She felt for a pulse. There was none. Gavin was dead. Recently dead, because the body was still warm, the blood fresh.

Helen sat back on her heels, and looked around the room, puzzled and aghast. It was Annie's room; aside from the few recent signs of Gavin's presence — an empty soup bowl on top the nightstand, a gum wrapper that had apparently been tossed at a waste basket and had ended up on the floor instead, a rumpled bedspread — aside from them, the room had a strange unlived-in look to it.

A small television set sat atop the dresser. It was on, the volume turned down low, although perhaps it had been intended to cover any other sounds anyone might have made.

But what the room lacked, what really jumped out at her now, was any sign of girlish occupation, the sort of things to be seen in most young girls' rooms. No dolls displayed atop the bedspread, no frilly dressing table. Really, there were no frills at all. No rock posters on the walls. It had an air of loneliness.

As Gavin must have felt lonely, even in the arms of his mistress. A mistress who, after all, could never be his, not so long as her husband remained alive. Gemma Hurst would certainly never have abandoned her crippled husband. Had Gavin ever, Helen wondered, contemplated ending the husband's life? Perhaps he had chosen ending his own as the better alternative. Might his death have been suicide?

She looked again at the body lying on the floor. He looked smaller than Helen remembered, as if the wound in his forehead had somehow shrunk him. Death often did that, it seemed to her. Dead people never looked as large as they had in life. Maybe, she thought, life itself filled you up, like helium in a balloon: stretched you out to the max.

Gemma Hurst had been right when she had said she would never see him again. If his death was suicide, maybe she had even driven him to it. Love and pity made a terrible brew together, when hope was left out of the recipe.

And she thought that surely Gemma had given up hope. Probably they both had, which was what had made it so poisonous. But it was Gavin who had paid the ultimate price.

Or had he? Maybe, she thought, Gavin had just finally gotten free. Living with failure could be even worse than death. When things did not get right, they tended to fester. And most likely, things were never going to get right for Gavin again. A gun had offered a simpler solution.

But a gun was only a tool, no better nor worse than a screwdriver or a pair of pliers; until it had killed someone. Then it assumed an aura of its own, an evil aura. After that, it was never just a tool again.

Then it came to her out of the blue: If Gavin's death had been a suicide the gun with which he had shot himself would still be here. Her eyes combed the floor around the body, to be sure, but she saw no gun. You couldn't shoot yourself dead and then hide the gun after you had drawn your last breath.

But if the gun was not here it meant someone else had shot him. Making it murder, then, not suicide. Which definitely changed the entire picture, and not for the better, either.

She thought of the ceiling light, turned off when she came into the room. Surely Annie had said it was on. Which could only mean the murderer had turned it off. And that shot she had heard . . .

All of which meant, unless her thinking had gotten very muddled, Gavin had been murdered, by someone right here in the house. Only minutes before. Someone with a gun. Someone who presumably still had that gun.

Doug? He'd had a gun earlier, had threatened to shoot Gavin on sight. Had he somehow come into this room, found the object of his threats watching television here, and carried those threats out?

But was she sure the gun was not here? Alarmed with this new direction her thoughts had taken, Helen jumped to her feet, thinking to make a better search for the gun.

She started to turn but there was another loud report. Someone slamming a door? Or a gunshot? Helen felt a horrible searing sensation along the side of her head. She took a step toward the open door to Annie's room. She had an impression someone was standing there, but she couldn't be sure. Her eyes refused to focus. It was as if she saw everything through a curtain. A blood red curtain.

'What ... ' She muttered, and collapsed in a heap on the floor beside Gavin's body.

17

Helen came out of unconsciousness slowly, confusedly. There were lights, bright lights, shining down on her from above. Was she in Heaven?

She tried to open her eyes, and discovered that one of them, the left one, was covered with something. She forced the other eye open. She was lying in a bed. The ceiling light was painfully bright.

'You're awake,' a familiar voice said. Helen relaxed a little bit. That was Jake's voice. Jake was there. Everything would be okay. Jake would not let anything bad happen to her.

'She's awake?' Another voice asked.

Helen frowned. The voice was familiar, but she couldn't quite place it. She saw Chief Tyler standing alongside the bed, but behind Jake.

'I need to talk to her,' Tyler said when he saw the open eye looking up at him.

'She's been shot,' Jake said.

'I am?' Helen said, surprised. 'I was?'

'You were,' Jake said.

'Am I dead?'

Jake laughed. 'No, you aren't, but it was close. Luckily whoever did it was a lousy shot. The bullet grazed your head.'

'I think I'm blind. I can't see,' Helen said. 'Not out of the left eye, anyway.'

'It's bandaged,' Jake said.

The door to Helen's room opened and a nurse came in. She frowned at his visitors. 'Three of you? I don't think any of you are supposed to be in here, let alone three of you,' she said.

Three? Helen had only counted two. She managed to lean her head to the side. Annie was standing by the door. She smiled weakly and waggled her fingers.

Tyler fumbled his badge out of a pocket. 'Police,' he told the nurse. 'I need to talk to your patient.'

'I'm with him,' Jake said, indicating Tyler.

Annie said, 'I'm with them.'

'I don't think . . . ' the nurse started to say.

'Uh, Ms. Nightingale,' Helen intervened.

'They're here to give me comfort, which I sorely need. But I'm guessing from your uniform that you are part of the medical staff. So, tell me, how am I? What's the prognosis?'

'It's up to the doctor to tell you that,' she said in a businesslike voice.

'Who is not here, but you are,' Helen said. She added, in a wheedling voice, 'And I won't squeal, I promise.'

'I can't . . . '

'Ah, come on. At least tell me if I'm going to lose this eye. I'm scared.'

'Well . . . ' she took the chart from the foot of the bed. 'You'll have to act surprised when the doctor comes in, like you've never heard any of this before.'

'Nobody does surprise better than me,' Helen assured her. 'You should see me at parties. The eye?'

'Is fine. The wound on the side of your head is only superficial, but the eye got a lot of blood. The bandage is just a precaution. And it looks like you've got a concussion.'

'No surprise there,' Jake said.

'Apart from that, I would say you're

going to be fine.'

'No thanks to whoever shot you,' Jake said.

'Did you get a look at him?' Tyler asked.

'Yes, and no,' Helen said. 'I saw someone at the door, but just for a second or so. At least, I thought I did, but they were more like a shadow. I have no clue who it was. If it was even anybody. It's all kind of a blur.'

'Interesting,' Chief Tyler said. 'But it doesn't help me solve my murder.'

'Two murders,' Helen said. 'Gavin was shot too. He didn't get off as lucky as I did.'

'You're right, he didn't. If he was murdered,' Tyler said. 'I was thinking of my sister's death.'

'*If* he was murdered?' Helen repeated.

'The jury's still out on that one. But not on Lois's death, I think.'

'For which everyone wants to blame Gavin Rand,' Helen said. 'But he could not have murdered Aunt Lois . . . '

'She was not your aunt,' Police Chief Tyler said crisply, interrupting her.

'I know that. It's just what I've always called her. Anyway, he could not have been the one who did that, because Gavin was in the house in Burbank, the whole time since we arrived yesterday.'

'And you know that because . . . ?' Tyler raised a questioning eyebrow.

'That he was at the house?' Helen looked surprised by the question 'Because Annie was there too. She is his witness.'

'But I'm not,' Annie said shamefacedly, stepping forward. 'I wish I was, but I was out in the front room much of the time. Alone. I only saw him twice. Once, when I went in there, into your bedroom, and he was sleeping in your bed, and later, when he came out where I was, wearing his boxers.'

'Well, then . . . ' Helen sputtered. 'Jake and I can alibi him. We were right there on the floor, beside the bed. While he was sleeping. Beside him.'

'Let me ask you,' Tyler said. 'Were you aware of his coming out of there the time Annie mentions, in his boxers?'

'No, I . . . he must have stepped right over us.'

'Without waking you?'

'I sleep soundly,' Jake said.

'We both do,' Helen agreed. 'After we . . . well, we both are sound sleepers.'

'I see. So the fact is, he could have stepped over you twice, or three or four times, without your knowing it, isn't that so? For all you can say, he might have gone out, gone to the hospital, murdered my sister, and come home and climbed right back into bed, and you'd never have known he was out at all, would you?'

'And just how did he get to the hospital?' Helen demanded. 'Do you suppose he walked?'

'He walked to Burbank, didn't he? According to what Annie told me.'

'That's what they said,' Annie said.

'Well, sure. Most of the way,' Helen conceded. 'At least, that's what he told us.'

'But he has a bum foot,' Jake said. 'I think he was pretty well walked out by the time he got to Burbank. I can't see him doing much more walking.'

'Or he could have borrowed someone's car,' Tyler added.

'Whose?' Helen asked.

'I have no idea,' Tyler said. 'Maybe he borrowed a car from someone at the hospital. Maybe he hadn't walked there at all.'

'He was walking when we saw him. So what happened to the car?'

'Maybe it broke down. Or ran out of gas. How should I know?'

'Or maybe what he told us about walking was the truth,' Jake said.

'Okay, so let's say it was,' Tyler said. 'That still doesn't mean he could not have gotten to the hospital. Mister Carter's car is in the garage behind the house, a big old Caddy. And he says he leaves the keys in it. Gavin could have known that.'

Helen had to admit, even she had known that.

18

'But,' Helen argued, 'maybe Gavin did not know that. About Doug always leaving his keys in the car.'

By this time, they were back at the house in Burbank. Helen's doctor had insisted that she must stay overnight, maybe for two days. Helen had insisted she wanted to be discharged. Helen won. But now she felt like she was on stage, playing the part of a pirate, with a patch over one eye. Maybe Peter Pan?

'Everyone knows about the keys. Always did. I've never made a secret of it,' Doug said. 'I'm going to fix myself a martini.' He went to the bar and suited actions to words.

'But he couldn't have gone out without going past Annie,' Helen insisted. 'She was here.'

'The whole time?' Tyler asked her.

'Yes, of course,' Annie said, and then, quickly, 'No, not every single minute. I went to the bathroom, to the kitchen, I don't know, exactly. But I wasn't sitting on the sofa every single moment of the evening, no.'

'Meaning,' Tyler said, 'he could have waited upstairs until he saw her leave the room, and dashed outside, gotten the car from the garage . . . '

'She'd have heard him drive away,' Helen said. 'Wouldn't she? Wouldn't you?'

Tyler looked a question at Annie. Her response was a shrug. 'Maybe,' she said.

'Or maybe not.' Tyler sighed. Personally he was beginning to agree with these three. He thought Gavin Rand had been twice a victim: once, of his family, which probably meant, of his wife; and once of life in general.

But he couldn't see any way of proving that. The alibis these three were giving him were too full of holes; they would never stand up in a courtroom. And the young man's suicide itself spoke for the soundness of his mind. If it was suicide. He'd have to wait for the coroner to tell him that. But he couldn't help thinking it was likely.

He had begun to think, too, that there

was something wrong with Dee. Much of what she did was just for show. Like her anger. She made a big show sometimes of being angry, but it was more like her anger just rode the crest of her emotions, like a surfer riding a wave.

When people were genuinely angry, you could almost hear their anger seething through them. The way you could sometimes hear the energy humming through a power line. Dee's anger was showy, but it was superficial. Everything about her was, in his opinion.

But that was not a crime. He could not arrest her for it. In fact, he couldn't think of anything at all he could do about her. So far nothing she had done could have been said to break any laws.

Of course, the coroner was the one who would make the final determination about the dead man upstairs, but Tyler had to admit he had doubts. Was Gavin's death a murder as Helen, who admitted everything was blurry, seemed to believe, or, as Doug kept insisting, a suicide?

'Doug,' he said, 'you know, of course, that I'm going to have to have that gun of yours, to check it against the bullet that killed Gavin.'

'It's right there, in the credenza.' Doug pointed. 'Top right drawer.'

'But it isn't,' Tyler said. 'I've already looked.'

'Well, that's where I left it.'

'Maybe so, but it's gone now,' Tyler insisted.

'If it is, then I'd have to say the crazy man took it. To kill himself with.'

'If Gavin shot himself,' Helen said, 'Where is the gun? I didn't see one when I found the body. And the police haven't turned up one since.'

'Which only proves my point,' Doug said. 'Crazy people are sly. Everyone knows that.'

'He'd have to be a lot more than sly to disappear a gun after he had shot himself with it,' Helen said.

They were interrupted by the ringing of the doorbell. 'I'll get it,' Annie said, and ran up the steps to the foyer. She opened the door, to find Danton Rhodes standing there. They were both surprised to see one another.

'Danton!'

'I was expecting Dee,' he said.

'She's in her room.'

'You might as well come on in, Danton,' Tyler said. 'We were discussing the murder of my sister. Maybe you can shed some light on it.'

'Murder?' Danton looked surprised. 'The last I heard, she was in a coma.'

'Was,' Tyler said, 'Until somebody decided to kill her.'

'How . . . how,' Danton seemed to be trying to find the right word. 'How tragic,' he finally managed to say. 'But, you said, 'someone.' Surely it was the same one who beat her unconscious earlier. Dee's ex-husband, as I understood it.'

'My thoughts exactly,' Doug said from his position by the bar.

'Dee's late husband, you mean,' Helen said.

'He's dead too?' Danton asked. Helen nodded.

Danton looked appropriately startled by that news. 'But, how? How did he die?'

'We're still trying to work that out,' Tyler said.

Dee came to the top of the stairs just then and started down. She stopped when she saw Danton below.

'Danton,' she said, sounding confused.

'I came to pick you up,' he said, and after no more than a heartbeat, asked, 'Wasn't I supposed to?'

'Yes. Yes, of course,' she said. 'I'll just get my suitcase.' She turned and would have gone back upstairs, but Tyler stopped her.

'Suitcase? I hope you weren't planning on going anywhere.'

She looked down at him. 'As a matter of fact, I was. We were.'

'Your plans have been changed, then,' he said. 'Nobody is going anywhere until I have a few questions answered.'

'What questions?' she asked in a saucy tone.

'For starters, there's the question of what happened to my sister.'

'Lois? My stepmother, you mean?'

'She's dead, Dee,' Danton said, and his tone seemed to suggest something deeper than just passing on information."

'Yes, I heard that,' she said.

'And then there's the question of Gavin Rand. Your ex-husband, I believe, Dee,' Tyler said.

'Yes, ex is the operative word,' Dee said. 'Have you found him, then?'

'We have,' Tyler said.

'He's dead, too,' Helen said.

Dee stood where she was for a moment longer. Then she flounced the rest of the way down the stairs to join the group in the living room.

'Well, I hope no one is expecting me to mourn him,' she said.

'Aren't you even curious as to how he died?' Jake asked.

'Not really,' she said, and then added, 'But as a matter of curiosity only, how did he die?'

'From a gunshot,' Tyler said.

'Did he kill himself?' she asked.

'What makes you ask that?' Jake asked.

She shrugged eloquently. 'It wouldn't surprise me, is all. He was never what you would call a stable person.'

'I think someone else shot him,' Helen said.

'You think?' Dee raised her eyebrows.

'He did not seem to have a gun,' Helen said. 'Which would rule out suicide, I should think.'

'Except, you admit that none of what you remember is very clear,' Tyler said. 'Maybe the gun was there, and you overlooked it. Or you've just forgotten it?'

'Then where is it?' Helen asked. 'You've been up there, surely. Did you see a gun?'

'What about you?' Doug asked Helen.

'What about me?'

'What about the bullet you say you were shot with. Are they doing any ballistics tests on it?'

'No bullet,' Tyler said. 'Well, there was a bullet in the wall, which might or might not be the one that wounded Helen. If it was a bullet, and not just a bad fall. And, yes, we are testing it. But unless we find your gun, Doug, there's no way to tell if it was fired from that weapon or not. You see what I am saying?'

'I do, Chief, I truly do. But I can't help you. All I know is I left it in the credenza over there. If it's not there now, it means someone took it. Who?' He shrugged dramatically. 'How am I to say? The crazy man seems like the obvious choice to me.'

'I don't think Gavin was crazy,' Jake said. 'He was ill. He had cancer. So, he was terminally ill. But not crazy.'

'There you go,' Doug said. 'He was sick. And cancer can be a painful way to go. He knew he was going to die, probably in agony. Maybe he thought it was simpler just to make quick work of things.'

'You think he just plain went crazy?' Tyler asked. 'Is that what you're saying now?'

'Or maybe he just realized that the jig was up,' Doug said brutally. 'Doomsday.'

'Ragnarok, you mean?' Helen said, and when Doug gave him a puzzled look, added, 'Swedish. For Doomsday.'

'Too deep for me,' Dee said. 'And if you ask me, it sounds too deep for Gavin too. He wasn't a profound person, you know.'

'Maybe not, but he was a live one,' Helen said. 'And now he is not.'

'And you know nothing about any of this?' Tyler asked. He looked from Dee, who only batted her eyes fetchingly, to Danton, who paled, and said, 'What could I possibly know about any of it? I'm just a visitor here. An occasional visitor.'

'And Dee's fiancé,' Tyler said.

'That's true. But I still don't know anything about what goes on here in this house. Fiancé or not, I am an outsider.'

Tyler, Jake and Helen all three exchanged glances. They were all thinking the same thing: that Danton was lying. He knew something that he was not telling them. But what, exactly, Tyler wondered?

Doug shrugged and took a big swig of his martini. 'Whatever. To my way of thinking, I can't see that it makes any difference what anybody knew or didn't know. Gavin was a madman, everyone knew that.'

'I didn't,' Helen said.

Doug ignored her comment. 'Anyway, we were bound to find the man sooner or later. Sick or not, he would pay for his crimes. He knew that the same as everybody else. I think he just realized there was no way out of that corner in which he had painted himself.'

'But that still leaves the question, who shot Helen?' Jake asked.

'I would say the lunatic, if you want my opinion,' Doug said.

'But he was dead when I found him,' Helen cried.

'Was he?' Doug gave her a doubtful look.

'He was lying in a heap on the floor, with no pulse. That says dead to me,' Helen said.

'Of course, you're not a doctor,' Doug said.

'That's true. I'm not. Anyway, whoever shot me came in from the hall.'

Doug narrowed his eyes at her. 'You said you didn't see whoever it was.'

'I didn't. Well, I did, I think, but all I really saw was a blur.'

'So you don't know who it might have been. If there was even anyone there.'

'Besides, you still haven't explained what happened to the gun,' Helen said. 'I looked for it. Before I was shot. It wasn't anywhere near the body. So where was it?'

'How should I know?' Doug asked.

'Those guys are the detectives. All I know is what I know.'

Tyler turned his back on Doug. For the moment, that was only a physical gesture, symbolic; but it might come to something more than that. If someone other than Gavin Rand had taken the gun from the credenza, which seemed increasingly likely, it had to be someone here in the household, and there were very few apparent suspects. And whoever he ended up blaming for the theft would have to be arrested. But that almost certainly meant turning his back on Doug Carter; this time literally, not just symbolically. In which case, at best, he would certainly lose an old friendship.

But what action could he take? Despite the ongoing mystery of the gun's whereabouts, Gavin Rand might have committed suicide. There were plenty of reasons to suspect he had done so. And Helen by her own admission wasn't certain the gun hadn't been there. For that matter, had Helen even been shot? She had fallen. Maybe the wound had happened then. Or, maybe she had found the gun and somehow managed to shoot herself. People did, and not infrequently. In which case, she might not remember that.

It was certainly true that his sister had been murdered. But if Gavin Rand had not done that, who had? Surely not Dee. Despite his growing misgivings about Dee, Tyler could not bring himself to suspect her of murder. She might well be crazy. He had come to believe she really was at least a bit unbalanced. But the murder of his sister was not the sort of thing she could pull off.

Not that she was incapable of killing someone. That he could imagine easily enough. But if she did, it would be a spur of the moment thing, done in a flash of temper. Whoever had killed Lois had plotted out what they meant to do and then carried it through with ruthless determination. And the kind of patience and steadfastness that would be impossible for Dee to maintain. She was just too volatile. No, Lois's murder would have taken someone stubbornly committed to the deed.

'Whatever did happen to that house-keeper, by the way?' he suddenly asked aloud.

'Ricketts? She has a room, upstairs,' Annie said. 'I can show you, if you like.'

And what, Helen wondered, watching the two of them, was the explanation for the frightened looks Danton and Dee had exchanged just then. Had anybody else even seen the nervous glances, or Dee's almost imperceptible shake of her head?

'Burke,' Tyler addressed one of his men, 'go with her and see if the woman is there. If she is, I want to talk to her.'

'And if she isn't?' Burke asked.

'I still want to talk to her,' Tyler said. 'Wherever she is.'

'She went out earlier,' Grannie said. 'To the movies, I believe she said.'

'Has anyone seen her since?' Tyler asked.

'I haven't,' Dee said quickly; too quickly, Tyler thought.

'And I certainly haven't seen her,' Danton said. 'As everybody surely knows, I just got here.'

'I saw her,' Annie said. 'And so did you, Dee,' she added.

'Did I?' Dee's eyes were wide with innocence. 'I don't remember seeing her.'

'She came in when you were expressing your anger with me.' Annie had been about to say, 'having a tantrum,' but decided this was not the best time to make that kind of wave. It was almost certain to provoke yet another tantrum.

'Oh, you're right,' Dee said, sounding sulky. 'I had forgotten.'

'I saw her too,' Doug said, if a bit reluctantly. 'She was with you, Dee. Remember?' He finished off his martini and went to the bar to fix another one. Helen eyed him speculatively. Martinis tended to loosen the tongue. If Doug hadn't already polished off one, he would probably never have sided with Annie.

'I said I had forgotten,' Dee snapped. 'I can't remember everything that happens. I'm not a tape recorder, you know.'

'Come to think of it,' Doug said, pausing briefly to reflect, 'That was when I put the gun in the credenza. I believe.' He gave his oldest daughter a measuring look.

'If several of you saw the housekeeper

here, then she must have come home from those movies. Which means, she's got to be around here someplace,' Tyler said. 'If she's not in her room, find her,' he told Burke.

'Has anybody checked the cellar?' Helen asked, and saw Dee's eyes once again and very fleetingly flash with alarm.

'What makes you suggest that?' Tyler asked her.

Helen shrugged. What had made that pop into her mind? 'The key is not there now,' she said. 'I noticed it was missing when I came in earlier through the kitchen. But it was always just left in the door.' Tyler was looking hard at her.

'Check the cellar,' he told Burke. 'That's if she's not in her room.'

Burke and Annie climbed the stairs together, and came hurrying back down the stairs in no more than two minutes.

'Nobody there,' Burke said. 'Her room looks undisturbed.'

'Check the cellar,' Tyler said, nodding his head in that direction. 'Remember?'

'Right. Got it.' Burke went through the swinging door into the kitchen, and was back again in no time, almost running

'The cellar door is locked,' he informed his boss breathlessly.

'And no key?' Tyler asked.

'None. Not in the lock, at least.'

'It used to be kept there all the time,' Helen said.

'It's always been left there, in the door. Still is,' Grannie said. 'A burglar would have to get into the house first before he used that key. Anyway, there's nothing down there of any importance.'

'My mother's blackberry jam,' Dee said. Everyone looked at her. 'It was awfully good. I was very fond of it,' she said defensively.

'I find it hard to imagine a burglar going to all the trouble to break in here,' Grannie said, 'for a jar of blackberry jam.'

'Which does not explain the missing key,' Helen said.

'Or maybe it does. Someone must have removed it. Someone here. If everybody is right about it's always being there,' Tyler said to Helen.

Helen said confidently, 'And if someone removed it, they must have had a reason.

Grannie is right; they must have wanted something more than blackberry jam.'

'I certainly don't have it,' Dee said, although no one had asked her. She gave Danton another significant look.

'If Dee and I are not going to be allowed to leave for Mexico . . . ' Danton started to say.

'Nobody leaves town,' Tyler said.

'Then I think I might as well go home,' Danton said, and when Tyler frowned, he quickly said, 'It's just over the hill. Dee has the number, if you need me.' When Tyler gave him a quick nod, Danton fled.

'Is it my imagination,' Helen said to Dee, 'Or did you look relieved to see him go?'

'Me?' She turned innocent eyes on Helen. 'That's silly. No, it's beyond silly. It's downright crazy.'

'Why is it so crazy?' Helen asked.

'Why? I'll tell you why. Because we were supposed to be on our way to Mexico, Danton and me. To get married. And now he's gone home, and here I am stuck where I always am stuck.'

'You couldn't get married anyway,' Doug

said. 'Not with Lois just dead. How would it look? Your stepmother is murdered, and all you can think of is running off to Mexico to get married?'

'That's what Ricketts said,' Dee snapped. 'The very same thing.'

'When?' Helen asked. 'When did she say that?'

'She said it when . . . when . . . ' Dee hesitated and finished, sullenly, 'I don't remember when she said it. But she did. I remember that much.'

'She must have said it after Lois died,' Jake said.

Dee thought for a moment. 'No, now that I think of it, she didn't exactly say that. What she was talking about was Lois being in the hospital. What she said was that it wouldn't look right, me getting married while my stepmother was in the hospital.'

'Well, you're not going to Mexico, not today, anyway. And there must be another key to that cellar door somewhere,' Tyler said. 'Doug? Know where we could find one?'

'I don't think there is one,' Dee said,

and at almost the same moment, her grandmother said, 'There's one hanging in the closet in the kitchen. On the back of the door. On the nail.'

'Get it,' Tyler told Burke. 'And use it.' Burke hurried off again in the direction of the kitchen.

Doug gave him no more than a quick glance. He was convinced this was a fool's errand. What could anyone possibly find in the cellar, besides, as Dee had pointed out, some blackberry jam?

19

Ricketts had regained consciousness some time earlier, and found herself on the floor of the cellar, at the foot of the wooden stairs. She tried to sit up and a sharp stab of pain went through her left side. She moved that arm. Yes, it felt as if her shoulder was broken.

But where was the gun? Hadn't she had it earlier? She thought back. No, Dee had taken it from her. Before pushing her down the stairs.

She made the laborious climb on hands and knees, back up the stairs. It seemed to take forever to reach the landing at the top. She got to her knees and tried the knob, but just as she had suspected, the door was locked. She sat there, panting, her legs dangling over the stairs, and leaned her back against the closed door.

Her original intention had been to pound on the door until someone heard her and came to let her out. But on that long, laborious climb up the stairs, she'd had plenty of time to reconsider.

She was furious with Dee. She'd had every intention of telling everyone what had actually happened to her, about Dee tricking her, and then shoving her down the stairs. It would serve Dee right if everyone knew what she had done. It was wicked. She should know better than to betray her true friends, the ones who looked out for her.

But how could she tell anyone about that? Dee knew what she had done at the hospital, that she had murdered Lois. She had confessed the murder to Dee. And it was she who earlier had given Dee her advice about how to deal with her original attack on Lois, the one that had sent Lois to the hospital in the first place. About saying she had seen her ex-husband running away.

The truth was, when she looked back over the events of the last couple of days, she saw quite clearly that she was now at Dee's mercy. Doubly so, in fact. Dee was the only thing between her and going to prison, maybe even to the electric chair (Did they still use that? She had no idea. It had never crossed her mind until now that she needed to know such a thing.) If Dee started blabbing to people what she knew, prison was almost a certainty, for both of them. And for her, if not the chair, some lethal kind of punishment. Hanging? Gas? None of them sounded very cheery.

Worse yet, she had little hope that Dee would not talk. If she got angry, or excited, the girl had no sense at all. No matter if she incriminated herself by talking. She would never even pause to think of that. Thinking clearly was not Dee's strong suit.

To make things still worse, Ricketts had no idea how long she had even been in the cellar. She had no idea even what time it was now. She had a watch on her wrist, but she'd already noticed that had broken in her fall

She crouched down on the landing and put her ear to the crack at the bottom of the door. Yes, she could hear voices, but they were only a distant murmur. Too far away, in fact, for her to say whose voices they were. For all she could know, Dee might be spilling her guts at this very moment.

Spilling her guts, she thought, and mine. Mine worst of all.

She got back up and sat again, her back against the door. When it opened suddenly, it so surprised her that she actually fell into the kitchen, on her back.

'Found her,' a male voice called out. 'The housekeeper.'

Thinking again of Dee, of what she might do or say, Ricketts closed her eyes and pretended to be unconscious. She kept up the pretense when others came into the kitchen and gathered around her. She did not know how many others, and could not tell without peeking, but she sensed there were several of them. The air seemed crowded.

'We're going to need an ambulance,' a male voice said. Chief Tyler's voice, she thought. And someone else, Annie maybe, said, 'I'll call for one.' Not a peep out of Dee. Maybe, just maybe, she was in her room. If Ricketts could have her way, that's where Dee would stay. Locked in, to be safe.

Ricketts was not sure how long she had lain there on the kitchen floor, pretending to be unconscious. It seemed like it had been hours, but she knew perfectly well the mind could play tricks on you so far as the passage of time. More than likely it was no more than a few minutes. She thought she heard the distant wail of a siren.

Soon after that, someone lifted her onto a stretcher, and she was carried out; through the living room, she was sure, up the steps to the foyer. The change in the air told her that they had gone outside. Her eyes were still closed. They lifted her and slid her inside a vehicle, and the door was closed.

But they did not immediately drive away with her. She opened one eye cautiously and looked around. Yes, as she had supposed, she was in an ambulance. Which was not moving. But why not?

20

'Should we take her to the hospital?' The driver asked Tyler. 'She looks okay. I'm not even sure she's really unconscious, to tell you the truth. Her eyelids were fluttering, like maybe she was faking it.'

'In a couple of minutes,' Chief Tyler said. 'There are a few things I want to find out first. She may be going to the prison ward. Can you give me a little while?'

The driver looked in the direction of the ambulance. If he was wrong, he could lose his job, leaving an unconscious woman to just lie there. All of his training told him he should get her to a hospital, as quick as he could. All of his instincts told him, however, that the woman in the ambulance was faking it.

'Sure,' he said. 'But five minutes, max. Okay?'

'Five minutes,' Tyler agreed.

★　★　★

Dee had watched with anxious eyes as the EMTs carried a seemingly unconscious Ricketts through the living room and out the front door.

'Has she said anything?' she asked, and when no one answered her, she said, 'Is she talking at all?'

'The chief is with her,' Annie said.

'And Helen followed them out,' Jake added.

'Between the two of them, they ought to be able to figure things out,' Grannie said.

'What things?' Dee demanded. 'What's to figure out?'

'Well, for starters,' the old lady said, 'she did seem to be locked in the cellar. It does make one wonder how that happened.'

'Didn't she have a gun?' Dee asked. 'We know whose gun it was, don't we, Daddy? And where she got it.'

Doug looked appropriately abashed. 'I put it away,' he said.

'Oh, sure,' Dee said, 'in the drawer over there. We all saw you.'

'But she did not have the gun,' Jake

said. 'Or if she did, I didn't see it when they brought her through here. And it's not on the cellar landing. And I don't understand: why would she have had a gun anyway?'

'Why?' Dee's voice went up an octave. 'She wanted to deal with my ex-husband, that's why. The madman. I should think that would be self-evident.'

'Except your ex wasn't in the cellar, was he?' Jake said. 'He was upstairs, in Annie's room.'

'How would Ricketts have known that?' Dee asked. 'If she went down into the cellar with a gun, obviously that's where she thought he was.'

'But why would she have thought that?' Annie asked.

Dee was saved the necessity of making a reply: Helen and Chief Tyler came in just then from outside.

'How is she?' Dee asked, and in almost the same breath, 'Is she talking yet?'

'A little,' Helen lied.

Tyler shot her a quick look, but he did not challenge the lie. Better, he thought, to see where this leads us. He could always correct Helen later. For the moment, he was interested in what Dee had to say.

'What did she say?' Dee demanded. 'Is she saying I pushed her down the stairs? That's a lie. It's ridiculous.'

'Is it?' Helen asked.

'Of course it is. I have no idea why she would even say such a thing. All I can tell you is I did not push her. She's lying if she says I did.'

'She also says,' Helen said, 'that Gavin Rand was not the one who beat Lois unconscious.'

Chief Tyler gave her another searching look, but he continued his silence. Things seemed to be getting suddenly very interesting. Dee had a flustered look now.

'Oh.' Strangely enough, Dee appeared to be considering what Helen had said. 'It's true,' she suddenly said. 'It was Ricketts who did that.'

'Ricketts?' Her father gave her an astonished look.

'Why, for Heaven's sake?' Jake asked.

'Because . . . because . . . ' Dee stammered for a moment and then quickly

279

brightened. 'Why because she hated her, that's why. She always had hated Lois. And they were quarreling when it happened.'

'Quarreling about what?' Tyler asked her.

'Why, about Danton, it seemed to me, though I wasn't really paying much attention. I think it was just a basic animosity, you know the kind of thing I mean. People quarrel just to quarrel. It doesn't always matter much what they say. Only, Ricketts got so mad, she took that big urn that used to sit on the pedestal, right here, you remember that urn, don't you Granny?'

'I do,' the old lady said, 'it sat on a gray pedestal.'

'That's the one, the big lavender urn,' Dee said excitedly. 'And Ricketts was so angry, she grabbed the big urn and hit Lois in the head with it. And when Lois fell down, she jumped right on top of her and began beating her head on the floor. Until I made her stop.' She looked around the room. Everyone was staring at her. 'I was afraid she was going to kill her,' she added in a small voice.

'But you were the one who said you saw Gavin running away,' Annie said.

'I . . . I had to,' Dee said.

'Why?' Annie asked.

'Why, because . . . because . . . she made me say it, that's why. She said if I didn't do what she said, if I did not say what she told me to say, she'd beat me, too. She even threatened to kill me. I was so frightened I just did what she said.'

'That's why you pushed her down the cellar stairs, isn't it?' Helen said. 'You were frightened.'

'Yes, yes, I was so frightened,' Dee said excitedly. 'And she had the gun. I was sure she was going to shoot me. She said she would kill me.'

'And you believed her,' Jake said.

'I did. Of course I did. She had already killed my stepmother, Lois. In the hospital. She said that it would not do for Lois to wake up and tell anyone what had happened. She told me about that. She confessed. To killing Lois. She laughed about it. It was Ricketts, she's the one who did everything. And I was terrified. I had to do what she told me. Until I tricked her about the cellar. I told her Gavin was down there. I got the gun away from her, too. And when she went to investigate, I shoved her, and I locked the door so she couldn't get out. That was clever of me, wasn't it? Wasn't I clever?'

'Very clever,' Helen said.

Dee turned in a circle. Everyone was staring at her. Her father was crying, but silently, tears streaming down his cheeks.

'I'll call our doctor,' Grannie said, and got up laboriously from the sofa where she had been sitting. She gave Tyler a menacing look, though he had made no effort to stop her.

'She's not well,' she said, almost under her breath. 'Anyone can see that.'

The ambulance driver came in the front door just then. 'Chief,' he said, 'What about this woman outside? Should I continue to just wait? It's been five minutes.'

'No, I'm coming out,' Tyler said. 'I'll have to arrest her, to make it official. Then you can take her to the hospital. The prison ward. I'll have to question her when she's awake.'

'You ask me, I'd say she's awake now,' the driver said.

'That's as may be. If she's acting, we'll go along with the act for the present. She'll have plenty of time to answer questions.' He turned toward Dee. 'I'm afraid I'll have to arrest you, too, Dee, but we'll wait for your doctor. And,' he said to her grandmother, 'you should probably call a lawyer, too.'

'I intended to,' she said, giving the floor a good thump with her cane.

Helen was thinking, sometimes there is a moment when one's entire life changes, switches on its axis. Everything, your entire history, has been changed; it was as if you stepped from one universe into another, if the quantum people had it right.

Doug was sobbing loudly now. 'I messed up,' he cried aloud, although no one seemed to be paying him any attention. 'It's all my fault.'

Helen turned on him angrily. 'Stop it, Doug,' she ordered. 'You did your best. That's all anybody can do. You had the best of intentions, but life is just too random to count on that. There's an old Yiddish expression, 'Man plans, God laughs.' If we could hear him, I expect he's having quite a chuckle right now.'

Dee turned slowly around in another circle. Then she cried out, but not one of the screams she had resorted to before; this was like an animal cry, it started somewhere deep inside her and came out more a strangled sob than a shriek.

But Helen knew: sometimes all that a miracle required was just a little encouragement. Dee had killed Gavin, she was as sure of that now as she had ever been about anything. Probably she had not planned on doing so, it had just been her temper, flaring up, and the unfortunate fact of a gun in her hand. And Dee had tried to kill her too. Dee was the blur she thought she had seen in the doorway.

She looked at Tyler, and saw that the policeman had reached the same conclusion. Tyler nodded his head, almost imperceptibly.

If they searched Dee's room, they would surely find the gun there. As Tyler would do, probably sooner rather than later. And in time, she would trade her life for Gavin's. If she was not executed, the rest of her life would be in an asylum.

'It's okay, Dee,' Helen said, holding a hand out to her. 'You're going to be okay. Knots can be undone as well as tied. Let's see if we can't unsnarl a few of yours.'

'Maybe I can help,' Annie said, and came to stand with them. When all was said and done, Helen thought, smiling at her, revenge usually turned out to be a waste of energy.

Only, how had it taken her so long to understand that, and Annie seemed to have grasped it all at once?

We do hope that you have enjoyed reading this large print book.

Did you know that all of our titles are available for purchase?

We publish a wide range of high quality large print books including:
Romances, Mysteries, Classics
General Fiction
Non Fiction and Westerns

Special interest titles available in large print are:
The Little Oxford Dictionary
Music Book, Song Book
Hymn Book, Service Book

Also available from us courtesy of Oxford University Press:
Young Readers' Dictionary
(large print edition)
Young Readers' Thesaurus
(large print edition)

For further information or a free brochure, please contact us at:
Ulverscroft Large Print Books Ltd.,
The Green, Bradgate Road, Anstey,
Leicester, LE7 7FU, England.
Tel: (00 44) **0116 236 4325**
Fax: (00 44) **0116 234 0205**

Other titles in the
Linford Mystery Library:

SHERLOCK HOLMES: JOURNEYS BY TRAIN

N. M. Scott

In his capacity as a consulting detective, Sherlock Holmes and his companion Dr Watson invariably find themselves travelling a good deal by train, and it is this which links the seemingly disparate events in one of the most fraught episodes in Holmes's career. A 'wheelchair mob' plans a series of daring gem heists, and ghosts are allegedly committing theft! Amid murder, poisoning and séances, someone is also threatening the faithful landlady, Mrs Hudson. Can Holmes get to the bottom of the mystery and bring the criminals to justice?

CASEY AND THE LOST BOYS

Geraldine Ryan

As DI Casey Clunes investigates the whereabouts of a missing volunteer, the suspicious behaviour of a group of schoolboys begins to interrupt not only her work, but her home life too . . . In *The Other Diana*, a teacher reveals a long-kept secret, leading to the reopening of a twenty-year-old unsolved case involving a murdered girl . . . And in *After Phoebe*, Vonny is forced to take a job at Oxford University and confront the darkness of her past. But now, she feels the presence of something far more threatening than her memories . . .

WHO WAS SYLVIA?

Carol Cail

After Maxey releases the body of a stranger called Sylvia for burial, she is determined to publish an obituary for the woman in her newspaper, *The Blatant Regard*. As she investigates further into Sylvia's life, Maxey is also intrigued by a man's death in a mattress store fire, just half a block from her own apartment. But when Maxey disappears on Halloween, it's up to her business partner Scotty and her lover, Fire Marshall Calen Taylor, to sort the tricks from the treats as she tangles with undisguised death.

SCARECROW

Eaton K. Goldthwaite

A Navy vet thought to be dead approaches a plastic surgeon to be 'remade', planning take his place as heir to a textile mill. Henry Heath, plant manager of the mill, is plotting to take control of the company's stock shares, but playboy Ford Sheppard discovers the scheme and attempts to blackmail him. Then two murders occur within hours of one another — one victim is Ford, the other an artists' model and Heath's mistress. Who is to blame — and how is the strange disfigured man known as the scarecrow involved?